The Gift of Autumn

A collection of impressions dedicated to Autumn's bountiful gifts of plenty and dramatic beauty.

ACKNOWLEDGMENTS

Excerpts from the following works of John Burroughs: SQUIRRELS AND OTHER FUR-BEARERS; SIGNS AND SEASONS; BIRDS AND POETS; UNDER THE MAPLES; WINTER SUNSHINE; PEPACTON; WAYS OF NATURE; HARVEST OF A QUIET EYE; A YEAR IN THE FIELDS; WAKE-ROBIN. Reprinted by permission of Houghton Mifflin Company. WOODLAND HARVEST by Constance Conrader. From WISCONSIN - STATE FOR ALL SEASONS, Jill Dean and Susan Smith, Editors, Copyright © 1972 by Wisconsin Tales and Trails, Incorporated. GOALPOST by J. B. Gillette. From PASQUE PETALS, October 1964. Used by permission. APPLE CIDER by R. J. McGinnis. From THE GOOD OLD DAYS, edited and compiled by R. J. McGinnis. Copyright © 1960 by F and W Publishing Corporation. Specified excerpts by Sigurd F. Olson: "Autumn comes without warning . . ."; "When I look at my bag of wild rice . . ."; "There are many legends and stories . . ."; "Rice gathering was never work . . ." From SIGURD F. OLSON'S WILDERNESS DAYS, by Sigurd F. Olson. Copyright © 1972 by Sigurd F. Olson. Reprinted by permission of Alfred A. Knopf, Inc. Specified excerpts by Sigurd F. Olson: "It was a bright and sparkling morning . . ."; "The base of the leaf was yellowish green . . ."; "But along the roadsides . . ."; "In that little leaf . . ." From LISTENING POINT, by Sigurd F. Olson. Copyright © 1958 by Sigurd F. Olson. Reprinted by permission of Alfred A. Knopf, Inc. Specified excerpts by Sigurd F. Olson from "Wild Geese": "It was November . . ."; "Another time, when the sun was setting . . ."; "The sound grew louder . . ."; "The long skein of dots . . ." Excerpts from "Smoky Gold": "The leaves are gone from the hillsides . . ."; "It was late October . . .: "In the north . . ." From THE SINGING WILDERNESS, by Sigurd F. Olson. Copyright © 1956 by Sigurd F. Olson. Reprinted by permission of Alfred A. Knopf, Inc. SUGAR MAPLE by Donald Culross Peattie. From A NATURAL HISTORY OF TREES (1950) by Donald Culross Peattie. Reprinted by permission of Houghton Mifflin Company. THE RAPTURE OF THE YEAR and WHEN THE FROST IS ON THE PUNKIN by James Whitcomb Riley. From THE BIOGRAPHICAL EDITION OF THE COMPLETE WORKS OF JAMES WHITCOMB RILEY, Copyright 1913 by James Whitcomb Riley. Published by The Bobbs-Merrill Company, Inc. Excerpts by Edwin Way Teale: "I smiled a little ruefully . . ."; "Nearly as much as the scent of leaf fires . . ."; "To the red man . . ."; "We were also now in the wonderful month . . ." Reprinted by permission of DODD, MEAD & COMPANY, INC. from THE AMERICAN SEASONS by Edwin Way Teale. Copyright © 1950, 1951, 1956, 1957, 1960, 1965, 1976 by Edwin Way Teale. Excerpts by Edwin Way Teale: "Not only are birds . . ."; "This was September . . ."; "For autumn advances . . .";"The beauty of the summer . . ."; "All across the country . . ."; "The simplest of the autumn colors . . ."; "The yellow of autumn . . ."; "If the cell sap is acid . . ."; "With very few exceptions . . ."; "Occasionally as we wondered . . ."; "Again, it has been noticed . . ."; "At one time it was believed . . ." "That sleep, the deathlike torpor . . ."; "Although scientists have been studying . . ."; "Nor is the main cause . . ."; "That day started . . ."; "One after the other . . ."; "Indian summer . . ."; "Through the sunshine . . ."; "One of the annual signs of autumn . . ." Reprinted by permission of DODD, MEAD & COMPANY, INC. from AUTUMN ACROSS AMERICA by Edwin Way Teale. Copyright © 1950, 1951, 1956 by Edwin Way Teale. Excerpts from the works of Henry David Thoreau, published by Houghton Mifflin Company. "I can see the woods in their summer dress . . ." by Mark Twain. Specified material from THE AUTOBIOGRAPHY OF MARK TWAIN edited by Charles Neider. Copyright © 1959 by Charles Neider. Reprinted by permission of Harper & Row, Publishers, Inc. WEATHER SIGNS. Excerpted from "Weather Signs," from THE FOXFIRE BOOK, Edited with an introduction by Eliot Wigginton. Copyright © 1968, 1969, 1970, 1971, 1972 by The Foxfire Fund, Inc. Reprinted by permission of Doubleday & Company, Inc. THE FIRST THANKSGIVING by George F. Willison. From SAINTS AND STRANGERS, Copyright © 1945 by George F. Willison. Used by permission of Mrs. George F. Willison. Recipes by Naomi Arbit and June Turner from HAVE A GOURMET CHRISTMAS; recipes by Aline Becker from WHOLE GRAIN COOKBOOK; recipe by Sally Manesberg Flanzer from FESTIVE PARTY COOKBOOK; recipe by Cyndee Kannenberg from NICE AND EASY DESSERTS; recipes by Darlene Kronschnabel from COUNTRY BREAD COOKBOOK, COUNTRY KITCHEN COOKBOOK and various issues of COUNTRY SCENE; recipe by Sophie Kuy from FAMILY FAVORITES COOKBOOK; recipes by Donna M. Paananen from MEATLESS MEALS COOKBOOK and NATURALLY NUTRITIOUS; recipes by Catharine P. Smith from FROM MAMA'S HONEY JAR; recipe by Gertrude Wright from SIMPLY DELICIOUS.

PHOTO CREDITS

Gene Ahrens, 50, 59; Alpha Photo, 7; Ed Cooper, cover, 4, 49, 52, 60, (top), 80; Ken Dequaine, 16; Fred Dole, 56; Olive Glasgow, 72; Grant Heilman, 3, 6, 29, 62, 67, 70, 74, 78; Gerald Koser, 24, 28, 32, 36, 39, 40, 41, 44, 47; Luoma Photo, 54; Milwaukee Public Museum, 17, 18 (2), 20, 22; Josef Muench, 8, 60 (bottom); National Park Service, 68; Tom Stack, 1, 76; Wisconsin Division of Tourism 12, 21, 64.

ISBN 0-89542-072-4 495

Editorial Director, James Kuse

Managing Editor, Ralph Luedtke

Production Editor/Manager, Richard Lawson

Photographic Editor, Gerald Koser

Copy Editor, Sharon Style

designed and edited by
David Schansberg

It was a bright and sparkling morning in late August with just enough hint of frost in the air to make one question the permanence of summer. A blue jay screamed the hard clarion notes of coming fall, and in that sound was the promise of change.

Sigurd F. Olson

Autumn

Autumn comes without warning at a time when the lush fruitful days of midsummer are beginning to wane, but when it still seems as though food, endless plenty, and warmth must go on forever. It may announce itself with just a touch of coolness on some bright morning toward the end of August, or by a few high leaves barely tinted with color, perhaps a spot of rusty gold on the bracken, or a tuft of grass turning sere. All young are grown now, ready to leave nests, spawning beds, dens, and shelters. Then, almost imperceptibly, a burst of activity is evident in a growing urge to store food, in a scrambling for seeds, cones, and dried fungi, and in the mounting piles of birch and aspen branches around beaver houses. New birds appear, gathering for the migration south, and there is excitement in the air with strange wings at dusk over marshes and lakes, and in the sense of little time and that all must hurry before it is too late.

Woven through all this is the dramatic phenomenon of color—at first hints and flecks of it floating in the gloom of the woods, then the bright and pastel shades of shrubs beneath the trees, and at last the trees themselves in such flaming magnificence it is almost more than can be borne. The north becomes a land of blue and gold, and skies once more are alive with the movement of myriad birds.

At last all the flamboyant beauty is on the ground, on portages and in pools and along lake shores. A somberness comes to the land and with it a feeling of welcome quiet and relief to all living creatures who stay on.

Sigurd F. Olson

In the fall the battles of the spring are fought over again, beginning at the other or little end of the series. There is the same advance and retreat, with many feints and alarms, between the contending forces, that was witnessed in April and May. The spring comes like a tide running against a strong wind; it is ever beaten back, but ever gaining ground, with now and then a mad "push upon the land" as if to overcome its antagonist at one blow. The cold from the north encroaches upon us in about the same fashion. In September or early in October it usually makes a big stride forward and blackens all the more delicate plants, and hastens the "mortal ripening" of the foliage of the trees, but it is presently beaten back again, and the genial warmth repossesses the land.

Before long, however, the cold returns to the charge with augmented forces and gains much ground.

The course of the seasons never does run smooth, owing to the unequal distribution of land and water, mountain, wood, and plain.

John Burroughs

This was September. This was the first of the "ber" months of fall. Name aloud the twelve months of the year and you will find that the four that comprise autumn, the only months that end in "ber," have the most round and melodious sounds of all—September, October, November, December. And three of the four, appropriately for a time when the fires of the year are dying down, end in "ember."

Edwin Way Teale

September

Sweet is the voice that calls
From babbling waterfalls
In meadows where the downy seeds are flying;
And soft the breezes blow,
And eddying come and go,
In faded gardens where the rose is dying.

Among the stubbled corn
The blithe quail pipes at morn,
The merry partridge drums in hidden places;
And glittering insects gleam
Above the reedy stream
Where busy spiders spin their filmy laces.

At eve, cool shadows fall
Across the garden wall,
And on the clustered grapes to purple turning;
And pearly vapors lie
Along the eastern sky,
Where the broad harvest moon is redly burning.

Ah, soon on field and hill
The winds shall whistle chill,
And patriarch swallows call their flocks together,
To fly from frost and snow,
And seek for lands where blow
The fairer blossoms of a balmier weather.

The pollen-dusted bees
Search for the honey-lees
That linger in the last flowers of September;
While plaintive mourning doves
Coo sadly to their loves
Of the dead summer they so well remember.

The cricket chirps all day,
"O fairest Summer, stay!"
The squirrel eyes askance the chestnuts browning;
The wildfowl fly afar
Above the foamy bar,
And hasten southward ere the skies are frowning.

George Arnold

I smiled a little ruefully at the recollection of one of my first discoveries in natural history made here in the fall. I was, at the time, in second grade. The teacher asked us to bring in brilliant autumn leaves and I found the most brilliant of all on a slope of the gravel pit. I knew my moment of triumph when I handed the large bouquet to the teacher. But it was short-lived. A few days later I was not at school. Neither was the teacher. For the bright-colored leaves were the autumn foliage of the poison ivy.

Edwin Way Teale

To return a little, September may be described as the month of tall weeds. Where they have been suffered to stand, along fences,

by roadsides, and in forgotten corners— redroot, pigweed, ragweed, vervain, goldenrod, burdock, elecampane, thistles, teasels, nettles, asters, etc.—how they lift themselves up as if not afraid to be seen now! They are all outlaws; every man's hand is against them; yet how surely they hold their own! They love the roadside, because here they are comparatively safe; and ragged and dusty, like the common tramps that they are, they form one of the characteristic features of early fall.

John Burroughs

How rich in color, before the big show of the tree foliage has commenced, our roadsides are in places in early autumn—rich to the eye that goes hurriedly by and does not look too closely—with the profusion of goldenrod and blue and purple asters dashed in upon here and there with the crimson leaves of the dwarf sumac; and at intervals, rising out of the fence corner or crowning a ledge of rocks, the dark green of the cedars with the still fire of the woodbine at its heart. I wonder if the waysides of other lands present any analogous spectacles at this season.

John Burroughs

By the first of August it is fairly one o'clock. The lustre of the season begins to dim, the foliage of the trees and woods to tarnish, the plumage of the birds to fade, and their songs to cease. The hints of approaching fall are on every hand. How suggestive this thistledown, for instance, which, as I sit by the open window, comes in and brushes softly across my hand! The first snowflake tells of winter not more plainly than this driving down heralds the approach of fall. Come here, my fairy, and tell me whence you come and whither you go? What brings you to port here, you gossamer ship sailing the great sea? How exquisitely frail and delicate! One of the lightest things in nature; so light that in the closed room here it will hardly rest in my open palm. A feather is a clod beside it. Only a spider's web will hold it; coarser objects have no power over it. Caught in the upper currents of the air and rising above the clouds, it might sail perpetually. Indeed, one fancies it might almost traverse the interstellar ether and drive against the stars. And every thistlehead by the roadside holds hundreds of these sky rovers—imprisoned

Ariels unable to set themselves free. Their liberation may be by the shock of the wind or the rude contact of cattle, but it is oftener the work of the goldfinch with its complaining brood. The seed of the thistle is the proper food of this bird, and in obtaining it myriads of these winged creatures are scattered to the breeze. Each one is fraught with a seed which it exists to sow, but its wild careering and soaring does not fairly begin till its burden is dropped and its spheral form is complete. The seeds of many plants and trees are disseminated through the agency of birds; but the thistle furnishes its own birds—flocks of them, with wings more ethereal and tireless than were ever given to mortal creature. From the pains nature thus takes to sow the thistle broadcast over the land, it might be expected to be one of the most troublesome and abundant of weeds. But such is not the case, the more pernicious and baffling weeds, like snapdragon or blind nettles, being more local and restricted in their habits and unable to fly at all.

John Burroughs

The plant depends upon the wind to scatter its seeds; every one of these little vessels spreads a sail to the breeze, and it is necessary that they be launched above the grass and weeds, amid which they would be caught and held did the stalk not continue to grow and outstrip the rival vegetation. It is a curious instance of foresight in a weed.

John Burroughs

To Autumn

Season of mists and mellow fruitfulness!
Close bosom-friend of the maturing sun;
Conspiring with him how to load and bless
With fruit the vines that round the thatch-eave run;
To bend with apples the moss'd cottage-trees,
And fill all fruit with ripeness to the core;
To swell the gourd, and plump the hazel shells
With a sweet kernel; to set budding more,
And still more, later flowers for the bees,
Until they think warm days will never cease,
For summer has o'er-brimm'd their clammy cells.

Where are the songs of spring? Ay, where are they?
Think not of them, thou hast thy music too—
While barred clouds bloom the soft-dying day;
And touch the stubble plains with rosy hue;
Then in a wailful choir the small gnats mourn
Among the river swallows, borne aloft
Or sinking as the light wind lives or dies;
And full-grown lambs loud bleat from hilly bourn;
Hedge-crickets sing; and now with treble soft
The redbreast whistles from a garden croft;
And gathering swallows twitter in the skies.

John Keats

For autumn advances like the rising tide. It has its warmer days and its days of increasing chill. Its waves move forward, then retreat. But all the while its average progress—like that of ocean water rising to the flood—is set in one direction.

Edwin Way Teale

Though halcyon period of our autumn will always in some way be associated with the Indian. It is red and yellow and dusky like him. The smoke of his campfire seems again in the air. The memory of him pervades the woods. His plumes and moccasins and blanket of skins form just the costume the season demands. It was doubtless his chosen period. The gods smiled upon him then if ever. The time of the chase, the season of the buck and the doe and of the ripening of all forest fruits; the time when all men are incipient hunters,

7

Indian summer, that halcyon time of fall, comes in different years and in diverse parts of the country at varying times of October and November. It has no fixed date, no definite duration, this time of golden haze and glinting gossamer with its sense of drifting and reprieve. The very nearness of winter accentuates its charm.

Edwin Way Teale

We were also now in the wonderful month of October, that perfect month of fall. In October calm and sunny days prevail. High winds are almost unknown; thunderheads are rarely seen; the season of tempests and cyclones is virtually over. In October the same temperature is found over a greater portion of the United States than at any other time of year.

Edwin Way Teale

when the first frosts have given pungency to the air, when to be abroad on the hills or in the woods is a delight that both old and young feel—if the red aborigine ever had his summer of fullness and contentment, it must have been at this season, and it fitly bears his name.

John Burroughs

It is the Indian summer. The rising sun blazes through the misty air like a conflagration. A yellowish, smoky haze fills the atmosphere, and a filmy mist lies like a silver lining on the sky. The wind is soft and low. It wafts to us the odor of forest leaves, that hang wilted on the dripping branches, or drop into the stream. Their gorgeous tints are gone, as if the autumnal rains had washed them out. Orange, yellow and scarlet, all are changed to one melancholy russet hue. The birds, too, have taken wing, and have left their roofless dwellings. Not the whistle of a robin, not the twitter of an eavesdropping swallow, not the carol of one sweet, familiar voice. All gone. Only the dismal cawing of a crow, as he sits and curses that the harvest is over; or the chit-chat of an idle squirrel, the noisy denizen of a hollow tree, the mendicant friar of a large parish, the absolute monarch of a dozen acorns.

Henry Wadsworth Longfellow

October's Bright Blue Weather

O suns and skies and clouds of June,
And flowers of June together,
Ye cannot rival for one hour
October's bright blue weather.

When loud the humblebee makes haste,
Belated, thriftless vagrant,
And goldenrod is dying fast,
And lanes with grapes are fragrant;

When gentians roll their fringes tight,
To save them for the morning,
And chestnuts fall from satin burrs
Without a sound of warning;

When on the ground red apples lie
In piles like jewels shining,
And redder still on old stone walls
Are leaves of woodbine twining;

When all the lovely wayside things
Their white-winged seeds are sowing,
And in the fields, still green and fair,
Late aftermaths are growing;

When springs run low, and on the brooks,
In idle golden freighting,
Bright leaves sink noiseless in the hush
Of woods, for winter waiting;

When comrades seek sweet country haunts,
By twos and twos together,
And count like misers, hour by hour,
October's bright blue weather.

O suns and skies and flowers of June,
Count all your boasts together,
Love loveth best of all the year
October's bright blue weather.

Helen Hunt Jackson

A clear, crispy day—dry and breezy air, full of oxygen. Out of the sane, silent, beauteous miracles that envelope and fuse me—trees, water, grass, sunlight, and early frost—the one I am looking at most today is the sky. It has that delicate, transparent blue, peculiar to autumn, and the only clouds are little or larger white ones, giving their still and spiritual motion to the great concave. All through the earlier day (say from 7 to 11) it keeps a pure, yet vivid blue. But as noon approaches the color gets lighter, quite gray for two or three hours—then still paler for a spell, till sundown—which last I watch dazzling through the interstices of a knoll of big trees—darts of fire and a gorgeous show of light-yellow, liver-color and red, with a vast silver glaze askant on the water—the transparent shadows, shafts, sparkle, and vivid colors beyond all the paintings ever made.

I don't know what or how, but it seems to me mostly owing to these skies, (every now and then I think, while I have of course seen them every day of my life, I never really saw the skies before,) have had this autumn some wondrously contented hours—may I not say perfectly happy ones?

Walt Whitman

Another perfect Indian summer day. Some small bushy white asters still survive.

The autumnal tints grow gradually darker and duller, but not less rich to my eye. And now a hillside near the river exhibits the darkest, crispy reds and browns of every hue, all agreeably blended. At the foot, next the meadow, stands a front rank of smoke-like maples bare of leaves, intermixed with yellow birches. Higher up, are red oaks of various shades of dull red, with yellowish, perhaps black oaks intermixed, and walnuts, now brown, and near the hilltop, or rising above the rest, perhaps, a still yellow oak, and here and there amid the rest or in the foreground on the meadow, dull ashy salmon-colored white oaks large and small, all these contrasting with the clear liquid, sempiternal green of pines.

Henry David Thoreau

After School in Autumn

Remember walking home from school on
  a warm October day . . .
How the maple leaves all red and gold
  were strewn along the way?
How they floated down from spreading
  bowers that lined the avenues,
And calicoed the paths around like
  quilts of patchwork hues?
Remember wandering slowly home in
  the Indian summertime . . .
How the crunchy leaves had a woodsy
  smell and the air was so divine?
And remember how we shoved those
  leaves into enormous fluffy heaps,
Then ran and squashed those leaf hills
  down in joyful flying leaps?
Remember loitering on the way . . .
  seems the years have turned to ages . . .

And reverently picking perfect leaves to
  press in school book pages?
Remember the football games we watched
  at the old athletic field . . .
How we stood in mud and rain and snow
  till our blood about congealed?
The big game of Thanksgiving? And the
  mud the players plowed?
How we cheered them on to victory and
  the songs we sang so loud?
As I watch the young ones coming home
  from school these autumn days,
Many things they do are related to our
  good old-fashioned ways.
How good it is to see the joys of old
  times still in favor,
To know that children of today like fun
  with old-time flavor.

Helen Shick

Even before the first school bells sound in September, a magical excitement begins to form. It starts in the hearts of boys and girls as they take to the practice fields to begin honing their athletic skills for the football season. Football is autumn's sport and it is magical in generating enthusiasm and emotion.

The excitement permeates the air over sandlots, high school fields, and college stadiums like a cool autumn mist. Soon the hometown paper and fans begin buzzing about this year's team and its chances of "going all the way." Anticipation and excitement grow as the important game with the crosstown rival approaches. By the time Homecoming arrives, wild fans will be chanting "We're number one!" across the country in a chorus of happiness and hope.

As Homecoming approaches girls rush to make sure their dresses are perfect for the dance. Floats are constructed and the band practices long and hard on their special half-time program. The day finally arrives, and the excitement spreads to the townspeople lining the streets to watch the parade. Many have come to catch a glimpse of the Homecoming Court or of a loved one in the parade, but most have come to cherish and relive a very special memory established by a Homecoming some years back.

The stands are packed with screaming fans anxiously awaiting the kickoff. The band and cheerleaders pump up the crowd with rousing songs and cheers. When the team sprints across the field, the excitement culminates into an eruption of cheers, claps, and confetti. A victory will carry the high spirits long into the night. Homecoming is here.

David Schansberg

Goalposts

Fall colors dot the landscape,
Homecoming Day is in the air,

Majorettes of golden cape
With batons poised, all debonaire,

The major tall in high cockade
Keeps pace with rolling drums,

With high school students on parade,
Mid smiling faces of alums,

It's a time to long remember,
With its air of cap and gown,

In the chill of late October,
Be those goalposts up or down.

J. B. Gillette

11

School Days

There is something exciting about September. You remember when the start of school meant a new pencil box. The deluxe model cost fifty cents and had compartments for pencils, pens, erasers, a pencil sharpener, and a folding aluminum drinking cup. The cover, which snapped down at the side, carried a band inside to hold a ruler.

Another memory is of tin lunch boxes with handles. Unlike the ones nowadays, they were basket-shaped, and sandwiches, cookies and fruit from their depths tasted especially good at noon hour.

A new plaid dress for a girl and a new shirt and jeans for a boy, with sturdy new shoes for both, were also customary.

With all this new equipment, we entered school to find ourselves one year older and wiser and one room higher in grade. New teachers . . . new friends . . . new studies. Yes, it was exciting, in a nice way.

Though times have changed, we wish the same feeling of adventure to the students of this September.

Esther York Burkholder

Still sits the schoolhouse by the road,
A ragged beggar sunning;
Around it still the sumachs grow,
And blackberry vines are running.

John Greenleaf Whittier

September

I love bright September,
The best month of all,
When trees don new dresses
And hickory nuts fall.

The clouds, soft as snowbanks
Drift through the skies;
The roadsides all flutter
With bright butterflies.

Way out in the orchard
The trees bow their heads
With apples so yellow
And apples so red.

I love bright September,
For each year it brings
New friends and teachers
And school bells that ring!

Ollie J. Robertson

One Room School

One, two, three, four
Walls, some windows and a door,
Some battered desks, a dunce's stool
Add up to the one-room school.

An iron stove that made us doze—
While one side baked, the other froze.
A teacher's desk, a hickory switch
That sometimes made our britches itch.

The teacher we all loved so well,
Who taught us how to add and spell.
From first grade on through graduation,
She nurtured our young education.

Though few there were in any grade,
We learned to be quite unafraid
Of what a higher grade might bring,
For each year we heard everything.

And if we could not spell a word
We should have learned while still in third
We could regain what we were missing
By knowing, later, when to listen.

We loved the little one-room school,
A citadel for sage and fool.
We learned of life, we learned endeavor,
But most, we learned to live together.

Martin T. Bergsjo

13

From Out of the Soil

Looking backward across the fields
As the sun drops in the west,
The farmer, tired but happy,
Turns toward home and needed rest.
First the faithful horses
Must be groomed with proper care,
Given refreshing drink and best of food.
For man, they did their share.

Tilling the ground and planting the seed,
Working from dawn until dark;
The creaking harness, the strain upon chain
To the song of the meadowlark.

The only sound that reaches his ear
As he plods through the heat of the day,
He feels the touch of the Hand of God
As he reverently bows to pray.

The life-giving seed, the fields well tilled,
He awaits and welcomes the showers;
He witnesses the miracle of creation,
In the warmth of the summer hours.
He sees fields of golden grain
Moving at the slightest breeze,
Reflecting the rays of the noonday sun,
Turning the whole into enchanted seas.

Contentedly he rests until the harvest moon
Calls him once again to the fields;
It is then he reaps a just reward
As he harvests what the good earth yields.
God expects us to do our part,
We cannot reap without toil,
But doing our share as man should do . . .
Great gifts come from out the soil.

R. H. Sotherland

The Huskers

It was late in mild October,
and the long autumnal rain
Had left the summer harvest-fields
all green with grass again;
The first sharp frosts had fallen,
leaving all the woodlands gay
With the hues of summer's rainbow,
or the meadow-flowers of May.

Through a thin, dry mist, that morning,
the sun rose broad and red,
At first a rayless disk of fire,
he brightened as he sped;
Yet even his noontide glory
fell chastened and subdued,
On the cornfields and the orchards
and softly pictured wood.

And all that quiet afternoon,
slow sloping to the night,
He wove with golden shuttle
the haze with yellow light;
Slanting through the painted beeches,
he glorified the hill;
And, beneath it, pond and meadow
lay brighter, greener still.

And shouting boys in woodland haunts
caught glimpses of that sky,
Flecked by the many-tinted leaves,
and laughed, they knew not why;
And schoolgirls, gay with aster-flowers,
beside the meadow brooks,
Mingled the glow of autumn
with the sunshine of sweet looks.

From spire and barn looked westerly
the patient weathercocks;
But even the birches on the hill
stood motionless as rocks.
No sound was in the woodlands,
save the squirrel's dropping shell,
And the yellow leaves among the boughs,
low rustling as they fell.

The summer grains were harvested;
the stubble-fields lay dry,
Where June winds rolled, in light and shade,
the pale green waves of rye;
But still, on gentle hillslopes,
in valleys fringed with wood,
Ungathered, bleaching in the sun,
the heavy corn crop stood.

Bent low, by autumn's wind and rain,
through husks that, dry and sere,
Unfolded from their ripened charge,
shone out the yellow ear;
Beneath the turnip lay concealed,
in many a verdant fold,
And glistened in the slanting light
the pumpkin's sphere of gold.

There wrought the busy harvesters;
and many a creaking wain
Bore slowly to the long barn floor
its load of husk and grain;
Till broad and red, as when he rose,
the sun sank down, at last,
And like a merry guest's farewell,
the day in brightness passed.

And lo! as through the western pines,
on meadow, stream, and pond,
Flamed the red radiance of a sky,
set all afire beyond,
Slowly o'er the eastern sea-bluffs
a milder glory shone,
And the sunset and the moonrise
were mingled into one!

As thus into the quiet night
the twilight lapsed away,
And deeper in the brightening moon
the tranquil shadows lay;
From many a brown old farmhouse,
and hamlet without name,
Their milking and their home-tasks done,
the merry huskers came.

Swung o'er the heaped-up harvest,
from pitchforks in the mow,
Shone dimly down the lanterns
on the pleasant scene below;
The growing pile of husks behind,
the golden ears before,
And laughing eyes and busy hands
and brown cheeks glimmering o'er.

Half hidden, in a quiet nook,
serene of look and heart,
Talking their old times over,
the old men sat apart;
While up and down the unhusked pile,
or nestling in its shade,
At hide-and-seek, with laugh and shout,
the happy children played.

Urged by the good host's daughter,
a maiden young and fair,
Lifting to light her sweet blue eyes
and pride of soft brown hair,
The master of the village school,
sleek of hair and smooth of tongue,
To the quaint tune of some old psalm,
a husking-ballad sung.

John Greenleaf Whittier

Rice gathering was never work, it was the occasion for a festival, with a sense of good feeling and industry that seemed to permeate the camp, the sea of tall grass out on the lake, and the very air itself.

Sigurd F. Olson

A Chippewa woman flails wild rice on a northern Wisconsin lake.

"Manomin"—Staple of the Indians

Wild rice or "manomin" was a staple in the diet of Indians throughout the marshy regions around the upper Great Lakes. Today, at about nine dollars a pound, wild rice is a luxury, served as a side dish with wild game, fish, or Thanksgiving turkey.

Wild rice was an important source of nourishment for the Indian; consequently the success of the rice harvest could spell the difference between starvation and plenty. The wild rice, after careful preparation, suited the Indian's nomadic life-style very well, because the grain could be stored indefinitely and transported conveniently.

Indians probably brought wild rice to the first Thanksgiving dinner to share with the colonists. The healthy nutrient was used for barter with voyagers, trappers, and explorers, who valued the distinctive taste as a welcome alternative to their dried corn and jerky diets.

The importance of wild rice to the Indian is reflected in some of the names they gave to lakes, rivers, or areas where the grain flourished. Variations of the word *manomin* appear in many Indian dialects. The name of Wisconsin's Menomini tribe translates literally to "wild rice people." Wisconsin has its Menominee County, Menominee River, and communities of Menomonie and Menomonee Falls. Even the name Wisconsin may have stemmed from association with the grain. Indians named this region Weese-coh-seh, or a "good place to live." A good place to live was considered a place where wild rice grew, and fish and game were plentiful.

The wild rice harvest was a time of enjoyment and celebration for the Indian. The harvest was conducted with care and was a matter of pride to the tribe. Each family or individual had a specific job for the harvest, and each executed his task with meticulous care, devotion, and artistry. Several tribes retain these customs today, because it is believed that a deviation from tribal custom would result in a loss of flavor, and the actual meaning of food and the harvest. Even commercial wild rice is harvested today by hand.

Each year at harvest time, a tribe would set up camp along the lakes and rivers where the valued crop was abundant. Few food supplies were taken because they could easily sustain themselves on the ripe kernels and game taken at the camp. Men hunted deer and rice-plump waterfowl, while women fished and dried the day's catch on long birch racks. Most of the rice harvesting was done by the more experienced women in the tribe. Canoes, propelled by long forked poles, slipped silently through the golden rice fields as startled waterfowl fled with their familiar clamor. The "ricer" would

bend several ripe stalks over the gunwales of the canoe, and with a smooth, almost simultaneous stroke, the stalks were flailed with a beating stick to release the long kernels. There was no wasted movement as the canoe slowly covered an entire bed. Even with extreme care about seventy-five percent of the rice was lost over the side to become next year's crop, or food for waterfowl. On good days, the women would return to camp several times with canoes loaded to the gunwales.

Now the rice had to be parched and threshed, two important activities reserved only for the most skilled craftsmen of the tribe. The kernels were spread on canvas to permit thorough drying; then dumped into a large kettle and placed over a carefully regulated slow fire for parching. Parching loosens the hard outer husks and gives a smoky flavor to the rice. Constant stirring was required to prevent scorching or burning.

The parched grain was placed in a large, entrenched tub. A sturdy log was erected about four feet above the tub. Treading was performed by a skilled young man wearing newly made deerskin moccasins for the occasion. With the graceful, precise movements of a dancer, the youth would carefully roll his feet over the rice, while supporting most of his weight on the log. The methodic footwork

A Chippewa man carefully threshes the wild rice kernels with his feet.

There are many legends and stories about how wild rice came to the Indian people, but there is one I like best. In the days of long ago, it was the custom for the chief to send young boys approaching manhood into the woods to live alone and prove their strength and courage. They existed on berries, roots, and anything they could find, and were told to stay out many days. Sometimes they wandered very far, got lost, and did not return. During these long and lonely journeys, spirits spoke to them and they had dreams and visions from which they often chose a name. If they returned, they became hunters and warriors, and in time took their places in the councils of the tribe.

One year, a young boy wandered farther from the village than all the rest. It was a bad time for berries and fruits and he was sick from eating the wrong kinds. This boy loved all that was beautiful and, though hungry, always looked about him for flowers and lovely plants. One night in a dream, he saw some tall, feathery grass growing in a river. More beautiful than any he had ever seen, it changed color in the wind like the waves on a lake. Upon awakening,

he went to the river and there was the grass, tall and shining in the sunlight. Though starved and weak, he was so impressed that he waded into the river, pulled some plants from the mud, wrapped their roots in moss and bark, and started at once toward the village.

After many days he saw the tepees before him, and when at last he showed what he had found, his people were happy and planted the still wet roots in a little lake nearby where the grass grew for several years until it became a waving field in the bay. One fall, a wise old Indian who had traveled in many countries and knew all things came to visit the village. He was taken to the lake to see the beautiful, tall grass one of the young men had found. Seeing it, he was amazed, raised his arms high and cried in a loud voice, "Manomen—Manomen—a gift from the Manito."

He explained that the seeds were good to eat, showed them how to gather the rice and separate the chaff from the grain. Before he left, he advised them to plant it everywhere, guard it well, and use it forever. The Indians have never forgotten—and now all over the north country it grows in golden fields.

Sigurd F. Olson

19

released the sharp hulls without damaging the tender kernels. The skill of the thresher was measured in the percentage of kernels left hulled and unbroken. The rice was then carried to an open area and spread thinly over animal hide for winnowing. The wind blew away the chaff and hull fragments, leaving the greenish black kernels clean and ready for use. The prepared rice was sewed tightly into bags and saved for winter food. A harvest celebration followed and the entire tribe participated in a dance and feast of game, fish, berries, and *manomin*, sustenance for the coming winter.

David Schansberg

Wild rice is not an ancestor of Asian rice. In fact, wild rice is not a rice at all; it is the kernel of a marsh grass. Native to North America, wild rice thrives in the glacial lakes and streams of the Great Lakes region.

When I look at my bag of wild rice, I feel rich. Food of the north, this is nature's wheat, the traditional staple of Indians in the lake states. True, they have many other foods, but this wild grain, gathered in the shallow, mud-bottomed lakes and rivers of the north Middle West, is more important to them than any other. Bloody tribal wars were once fought for its possession. Those whose lands included stands of it were considered wealthy and insured against starvation and want.

Wild rice is easy to prepare: it needs only to be washed, to have boiling water poured over it, and be allowed to steam to make it palatable. It should never be boiled, for that may result in a gray, gluey mass, unless it is mixed with meat or fat. As a stuffing for wild ducks, as a side dish, or cooked with game or fish it is superb. Even for breakfast, with berries, cream, and sugar, it could give modern cereals severe competition. It can even be popped like corn in a skillet, or mixed with bacon, mushrooms, or cheese. It can be served as an entire meal or in infinite combinations with other foods. A purely American dish, it is indigenous to the north . . .

When I see my bag of rice, I think of many things, for it holds far more than food. In addition to high nutrient value and flavor, it has certain intangible ingredients that have to do with memories, and for those who know the country where it grows and have taken part in the harvesting, it has powerful nostalgic associations that contribute as much to the welfare of the spirit as to the body.

Sigurd F. Olson

Roadside Stand

I love to visit roadside stands
  When autumn fills the air—
A grand array of sights and scents
  Is waiting for me there.

There are rosy, red-cheeked apples
  In baskets all around,
And bright orange pumpkins, big and small,
  Lie heaped upon the ground.

The jugs of cider stand in rows
  Like liquid burnished gold;
The Indian corn hung all about
  Is lovely to behold.

There's nothing I can think of that
  Can truly quite compare
With roadside stands in autumn and
  Their harvest beauty, rare.

Peggy Mlcuch

Apple Cider

Just before the first frost, we picked the choice apples and stored them in barrels in the cellar; then we gathered the windfalls and loaded them into the box bed of our farm wagon for the annual trip to the cider mill. My brother and I needed no prodding on this job. The Winesaps, Pippins, Northern Spies, Jonathans, Russets, and Rambos, and even the lowly Ben Davis, a good keeper but without sweetness, were thrown together into the wagon. Each added its delicate flavor to the blend. If an extra tang was wanted, a couple of bushels of crab apples were included. It was thought that late apples made the best cider; and they should be fully ripe, juicy and not "mealy." As we loaded the apples, we threw out the mushy ones.

As we jolted along the dusty road in the warm autumn sun the smell of apples lifted around us. If your nose was sharp you could pick out the peculiar perfume-like odor of the Delicious and the musky tang of the Russet. The apple smell clung to our clothes and bodies.

At the cider mill the wagon pulled up at the end of the waiting line of loaded wagons, the horses stomping and switching flies. There, the smell of fresh apples was enhanced by the fermenting pomace heap behind the mill. We climbed down and joined the other small boys around the free barrel, which sat in the shade near the press. There was a tin cup there, but we shunned this, for we had brought along our own supply of rye straws. Inserted in the bunghole, a straw was our preferred method of bringing cider to lip. It came up in just the right volume so that each sip could be rolled around the tongue and the full flavor enjoyed. When our bellies got tight we had to stop, but cider tasted good even after you were full. Of course, we had what grandfather called the "backhouse two-step" that evening, but it was worth it.

It was a long wait through the summer until the fall apples ripened, and one year my brother and I jumped the gun. We had a tree of early Yellow Transparent and another of a variety of small red apple we called the Strawberry. We gathered up the windfalls under the two trees, quartered the apples, and ground them in the sausage grinder. After we had two or three tubs of pulp we pressed out the juice in the sausage press. The press lacked the necessary high pressure, and we sprung the handle, but working most of the afternoon we turned out five gallons of what we regarded as excellent juice. Grandpa smacked his lips over it, too, but he took a dim view of the sprung handle and he showed us that we had squeezed only about half the juice out of the apples. "We'll get a regular cider press for you next year," he said.

The purpose of making cider in the old days was not primarily to supply a delightful beverage; cider was made then to supply the farm vinegar. Farmers have always found it difficult to keep sweet cider for any great length of time—it's just too darned good to drink. So those who wanted both vinegar and a drink made two barrels. The drinking cider was rolled into the cellar, a spigot hammered into one end, and a tin cup was hung on a convenient nail. Then the family went on an apple juice spree.

The barrel reserved for vinegar was rolled to the sunny side of the kitchen and there it remained until nature had taken her course with it. Then it was spigoted, set up on a platform, and referred to daily.

Cider is a profitable by-product for the fruit grower, for it uses culls and windfalls, which, like the cow's hide to the meat packer, is often the margin of profit. The fruit juice vitamin fad boosted cider sales, for cider is the cheapest of all commercial juices, and stands up favorably with citrus, berry, and grape.

Cider is made today in much the same way as it has always been made—apples are reduced to a pulp and the juice squeezed out. In the old days farmers with small orchards had hand presses of their own, but the community mill got the bulk of the crop.

The hand presses were simple—a grinder to chew up the apples and a press operated by a screw, both mounted on a wooden stand. The large presses had greater capacity, for water or steam power were substituted for hand power. The chief drawback of the small hand press is that it will not exhaust the pulp of all its juices. The first juice from a run is the free juice released as the apples are ground. This has no "body." As the pressure increases the juice gets heavier and more flavorful.

Cider made from a mixture of apples is better than that made from a single variety. For example, the juice from the Grimes Golden is almost colorless, and bland; from the Delicious very sweet.

At a power cider mill the apples are scooped into a hopper and from there are carried by a chain or belt conveyor to the grinder or chopper. The resultant mass of juice and pulp is about the consistency of thick applesauce. It includes skins, cores, seeds, and an occasional worm. A decayed spot in an apple discolors the cider and damages the flavor.

From the chopper the pulp falls into a bin directly above the press to await the pressing operation. A slatted wooden board is placed on the platform of the press, and a frame, with sides several inches high, set on the board. Then a cloth, made of burlap or similar material, is laid over the frame and the pulp is allowed to run out until the frame is heaping full. The cloth is folded over the pulp, corner-wise. Then the frame is lifted off, another slat board is placed over the first layer of pulp, followed by the frame and another cloth. The capacity of a hand press is 6 to 8 layers; that of a power press, 8 to 20 layers. This stack of prepared pulp is called a "cheese." The press is then set in operation, squeezing the juice out between the slatted boards and through the cloth. The juice runs into a trough at the base and thence

into a barrel or tank. It may pass first through a filter or clarifier.

A large hydraulic press will turn out 300 gallons at a pressing. A hand press, using a cheese from 6 to 8 layers, will turn out about 12 gallons at a pressing of from 4 to 5 bushels of apples. A hydraulic press will get 16 gallons of juice from the same apples.

After the cheese is devoid of its juices, the pomace, or "pummies" as the old-timers called them, are shaken out of the cloth. Today pomace is used as cow or hog feed, but formerly it was dumped behind the mill and was the source of a pungent, distinguished odor which covered the neighborhood. It is a legend that in one of these heaps of pomace, a "sport" seedling, later to produce the first Delicious apple, grew up.

R. J. McGinnis

APPLE CIDER PUNCH

4 c. apple cider
2 c. cranberry juice
1 c. orange juice
1 12-oz. can apricot nectar
1 c. sugar
2 sticks cinnamon

In a saucepan, combine all ingredients; heat and let simmer 20 minutes. Top punch bowl with floating orange slices decorated with cloves. Serves 20 to 25.

Mrs. Bennie Lovaasen

HOT MULLED CIDER

½ c. brown sugar
¼ t. salt
2 qts. cider
1 t. whole allspice
1 t. whole cloves
3-inch cinnamon sticks
Dash nutmeg

Combine brown sugar, salt, and cider. Tie spices in small cheesecloth bag; add to cider mixture. Slowly bring to boil; simmer, covered, about 20 minutes. Use cinnamon sticks as muddlers. Garnish with nutmeg. Makes 10 servings.

Darlene Kronschnabel

SPICED CIDER

1 T. sugar
1 qt. cider
1 lemon, thinly sliced
Peel of 1 orange and 1 lemon
1 stick cinnamon
1 whole nutmeg, crushed
6 cloves

In a large saucepan, mix all ingredients well; bring just to a boil. Immediately turn down heat and let simmer for 10 minutes. Strain and serve hot.

If you prefer, make this recipe a day ahead. Keep it chilled in the refrigerator and reheat just before serving. Garnish with lemon slices and cinnamon sticks.

Darlene Kronschnabel

When we think of autumn it is the apple that best captures, preserves, and symbolizes all the wealth and strength of this abundant season. Apples dominate the senses during the robust harvest days; the unmistakable "snap" of the ripe, succulent fruit; the pleasant fragrance and naturally sweet, refreshing taste; the rich, colorful sight of apple trees, row upon row, barely able to keep their heavily laden branches from touching the ground. The urgency of farmers to harvest the apples before frosts threaten the delicate fruit is mingled with the excitement generated at roadside stands by patrons milling over bushels

Autumn's Finest Treat

Although Americans no longer enjoy the plenty of the 1900s when nearly 1,000 varieties of apples came to market each season, we are not totally without diversity. Many of the more popular brands are still displayed and sold at orchards and roadside stands across the country. Brief descriptions of taste and use of these more popular varieties are listed below; however, the only real way to discover the wealth of distinctive tastes available each autumn is to go to the orchard and sample the fruit. Few experiences can be as rewarding and satisfying.

Variety	Description
Wealthy	tart, suitable for cooking, good for eating if fully ripe.
Jonathan	all-purpose, including good eating.
Delicious	desserts, salads.
Grimes Golden	excellent taste, desserts and cooking.
McIntosh	juicy, sweet, excellent eating, tends to disintegrate in cooking.
Cortland	excellent eating, all-purpose, not strong in character.
Golden Delicious	desserts.
Rhode Island Greening	tart, all cooking, best for pies.
Stayman Winesap	spicy, all-purpose.
York	keeps its shape, good for pies and all cooking where this is important.
Baldwin	all-purpose.
Rome Beauty	bland, but satisfactory for baked apples.
Northern Spy	superior for all purposes.
Yellow Pippin	tart, good cooking, desserts.

of ruby, golden, and green fruit, comparing, tasting, selecting, and simply enjoying one of autumn's finest treats. Autumn is for apples.

David Schansberg

The time for wild apples is the last of October and the first of November. They then get to be palatable, for they ripen late, and they are still perhaps as beautiful as ever. I make a great account of these fruits, which the farmers do not think it worth the while to gather—wild flavors of the Muse, vivacious and inspiriting. The farmer thinks that he has better in his barrels, but he is mistaken, unless he has a walker's appetite and imagination, neither of which can he have.

Such as grow quite wild, and are left out till the first of November, I presume that the owner does not mean to gather. They belong to children as wild as themselves—to certain active boys that I know—to the wild-eyed woman of the fields, to whom nothing comes amiss, who gleans after all the world, and, moreover, to us walkers. We have met with them, and they are ours.

Henry David Thoreau

Autumn Treats

GERMAN APPLE PANCAKE

6 eggs, separated
¼ c. flour
¼ c. melted butter
¼ c. milk
½ t. salt
3 apples, sliced

Beat egg yolks; mix in flour, butter, milk, and salt. Fold in the beaten egg whites. Heat 2 tablespoons butter in a large skillet; pour in batter. Top with apple slices. Cook over medium heat for about 5 minutes. Bake in a 400° oven for 15 minutes until golden brown. Top with sugar and cinnamon.

Gertrude Wright

SPECIAL APPLESAUCE

2½ lbs. cooking apples
2 c. water
¾ c. sugar
1 T. aromatic bitters

Wash, pare, quarter, and core apples. Add water; cook until nearly soft. Add sugar; cook a few minutes longer. Remove from heat. Add bitters; whip with wire whisk. Cool and serve. Makes about 2 quarts. Can be frozen.

Sophie Kay

APPLE CRUMBLE

4 c. chopped tart apples, cored, but unpeeled
1 t. lemon juice (if more tartness or flavor is desired)
½ c. honey (more or less, depending upon tartness of fruit)

Preheat oven to 350°. Place apples in a 9-inch pie plate. Pour honey over all. Pour Topping on fruit. Bake for 30 minutes or until fruit is tender when tested with a fork. Makes 8 servings.

Note: You can have fun experimenting with this easy-to-make crumble. For example, mix raisins with the fruit, mix raw sunflower or sesame seeds or chopped nuts into the topping, etc.

TOPPING

¼ c. brown sugar
¼ c. whole wheat flour
¼ c. raw wheat germ
¼ c. oatmeal
1 T. soy flour
1 t. nutritional yeast
1 t. cinnamon
¼ c. margarine or butter

Mix together dry ingredients. Cut in margarine until mixture resembles crumbs.

Donna M. Paananen

CHEESE-APPLE CRISP

6 medium apples (2 lbs.)
¼ c. water
2 t. lemon juice
1½ c. sugar or 2 c. white corn syrup
1 t. cinnamon
1 c. flour
⅓ t. salt
½ c. butter
⅜ lb. (1½ c.) grated cheese

Peel, quarter, core, slice apples. Arrange slices in a greased shallow baking dish. Add water and lemon juice. Mix sugar, cinnamon, flour, and salt. Work in butter to form a crumbly mixture. Grate cheese. Add to topping mixture and stir lightly. Spread mixture over apples and bake in a 350° oven until apples are tender and crust is crisp (about 30 to 35 minutes). Serve with Lemon Sauce or garnish with whipped cream.

LEMON SAUCE

½ c. sugar
1 T. cornstarch
1 c. boiling water
Salt
2 T. butter
1 T. grated lemon rind
2 T. lemon juice
Nutmeg

Mix sugar and cornstarch. Add the boiling water and a pinch of salt. Boil until thick and clear. Continue cooking in double boiler for 20 minutes. Remove from stove. Stir in butter and lemon rind and juice. A pinch of nutmeg may be added if desired.

Mrs. Lester Smith

APPLE SLICES

2½ c. sifted flour
1 T. sugar
1 t. salt
1 c. shortening
1 egg, separated
⅔ c. crushed cornflakes
5 c. sliced, peeled apples
1½ c. sugar
1 t. cinnamon
Milk

Sift together the flour, 1 tablespoon sugar, and salt. Cut in shortening with pastry blender. Put egg yolk in measuring cup and add enough milk to make 2/3 cup. Add to dry mixture. Mix just enough so dough shapes into a ball. Roll out half of dough to fit 15 x 11-inch baking sheet. Cover with cornflakes, then with apples. Mix 1½ cups sugar and the cinnamon; sprinkle over apples. Roll out other half of dough for top crust. Place over top of apples. Beat egg white until stiff and spread over top crust. Bake in a 375° oven for 40 minutes. Cut in squares.

Mrs. Paul J. Clark

Apple Butter

As the season progresses, the apple trees begin to give up their unharvested riches by cutting off moisture to the fruit, and weakening the stem connection; eventually the fruit will fall. In the past, and in some instances today, these apples are gathered to make apple butter—a delicacy spread on pancakes and hot biscuits during the cold winter months. When the maple syrup reserves from the spring begin to diminish, apple butter quickly became the household sugar staple.

In many rural communities apple butter making was, and still is, a social event as traditional as the quilting bee. Everyone helped and everyone reaped the rewards. Men and children gathered apples from beneath each tree in the orchards, and bushels of fallen fruit were loaded on horse-drawn wagons. A steady fire was built beneath a large kettle of apple cider and the fragrant juice was boiled until it reached the consistency of thin molasses. The cider was then cooled overnight.

As the cider boiled the women washed, peeled, and quartered the apples. Winesap, Cortland, Stayman, and Northern Spy varieties were generally used because they made tasty apple butter in any combination. The quartered apples were placed in the kettle with just enough water to start the cooking process. When the pot began to boil the mass was stirred constantly to prevent scorching. Apples cook down considerably, so a reserve of quartered apples was always on hand to insure a full kettle. When the apples achieved the appearance and consistency of applesauce, the cooled cider, was added along with sugar and spices. The spices were left to the discretion of the cook, but cinnamon, nutmeg, orange peels, ginger, or cloves were commonly used. The mixture was then boiled until it resembled the rich, deep brown color of coffee. Care was taken to reach the desired thickness, again depending on the personal preferences of the cook. Upon reaching the ideal taste, color, and consistency, the contents were removed from the fire and quickly preserved in crock jars to keep the luscious flavor throughout the long winter.

A feast, complete with plenty of fresh apple butter, followed the two days of tedious work and long hours. It was a well deserved reward long to be remembered by everyone.

David Schansberg

APPLE BUTTER

Wash and quarter enough apples to fill a 16-quart kettle. Add 2 cups of water. Cook slowly over very low heat and stir constantly. Use a heavy kettle with a broad, flat bottom to allow the apples to bubble freely. When they are thoroughly cooked, cool slightly. Run through a food mill. There should be about 8 quarts of pulp.

Measure 2 cups of sugar to 4 cups of apple pulp. Place mixture in a heavy kettle with a broad, flat bottom. Use a wooden spoon or a flat paddle to stir the mixture constantly while it is cooking over a very low heat. Add ten 2-inch sticks of cinnamon. To determine if apple butter is done, place some on a cool saucer. If no rim of liquid forms around the edge of butter, it is ready for the jar. Place in hot sterilized jars. Seal at once. Makes about 12 pints.

Darlene Kronschnabel

APPLE BROWN BETTY

4 c. soft bread cubes
½ c. melted butter
¾ t. cinnamon
⅛ t. salt
¾ c. brown sugar
4 c. peeled and chopped tart apples
  Ice cream

Mix the first 5 ingredients together. Arrange alternate layers of apples and bread mixture in a greased shallow 1-quart casserole. Cover with foil and bake in a 375° oven for 1 hour. Remove foil for last 15 minutes of baking time. Serve with ice cream. Serves 4.

Cyndee Kannenberg

APPLE CHUTNEY

To accompany a curry or just to sweeten up a meal.

3 lbs. green apples, cubed	½ t. salt
1 lime, cut up	1 t. cinnamon
1 orange, cut up	½ t. ground cloves
2 c. packed light brown sugar	¼ t. ground ginger
1½ c. golden raisins	¼ t. nutmeg
¼ c. cider vinegar	

Combine all ingredients in a heavy saucepan. Bring to a boil over medium heat. Lower heat to a simmer and cook for about 30 minutes, or until tender. Makes about 4 cups.

Naomi Arbit
June Turner

In October I went a-graping to the river meadows, and loaded myself with clusters more precious for their beauty and fragrance than for food. There, too, I admired, though I did not gather, the cranberries, small waxen gems, pendants of the meadow grass, pearly and red, which the farmer plucks with an ugly rake. . . .

Henry David Thoreau

Cranberry Harvest

The discovery of the tart, little berries traditionally served at Thanksgiving dinner is attributed to the Indian's keen eye for edible flora. The Indians were first to cultivate and harvest cranberries or "sassamanesh." The wild berries became a tasty condiment and an important food source to the Indian. They considered the bright crimson berries a symbol of peace; hence the reason for cranberries being served at the first Thanksgiving dinner. The Indians quickly taught the pilgrims how to use cranberries, making them a valuable trading commodity for the settler, who soon shipped the small delicate berries back to the motherland.

Cranberries could not be commercially grown in Europe because suitable growing conditions are unique to the acidic, water-logged peat bogs of New England and the upper Midwest. These bogs support very little other plant life, so cranberries have little competition for nutrients and light. Cranberry plants crisscross the bog with long horizontal runners which erect shoots that bear millions of pink, lightly scented flowers in late summer. In comparison with most fruit, the cranberry is a late developer. Small berries form; and as autumn temperatures begin to drop, the berries fade from green to white and finally ripen into crimson beauties in late October.

Commercial cranberry growing has become a major industry in the United States. As the berries begin to mature in early autumn, farmers must follow the weather very closely. When frost is imminent the cranberry bogs are flooded to submerge the plants and protect the fruit from freezing.

During the early days of cranberry farming, the fruit was handpicked and loaded into long, flat tubs pulled by horses with large wooden platforms tied to their hooves to prevent them from becoming mired in the bog. Now machines harvest the crop. Harvesting machines enter the flooded cranberry beds and flail the

vines, releasing the bouyant berries, which then float to the surface. In some areas the floating berries are deposited in special boats towed behind the harvesting machines. Another method of harvesting requires wader-clad workers to corral the berries into a corner of the bog where they can be raked onto the conveyor belt of a waiting truck.

Once the berries are harvested, they are shipped to processing plants for sorting and packaging. A resilience test determines the quality of the cranberries. A berry has seven chances to bounce over a wooden barrier and onto a sorting belt. If it fails to bounce, it becomes part of the "slush" pile. The bouncing berries are scrutinized by workers, all bruised and badly shaped fruit being discarded into the "slush" pile. The remaining cranberries are packaged; and many of them will undoubtedly flank roast turkeys across the country on Thanksgiving day. It's tradition.

David Schansberg

HOT CRANBERRY BUTTER

2 c. cranberries (fresh or frozen) ¼ c. brown sugar
1 c. granulated sugar ¼ c. butter
½ c. water

Combine cranberries, granulated sugar, and water in saucepan. Heat to boiling, stirring until sugar dissolves. Boil until berries pop (about 5 minutes). Add brown sugar and butter. Heat until dissolved. Serve hot with French toast, waffles, or pancakes.

Darlene Kronschnabel

CRANBERRY-ORANGE RELISH

4 c. fresh cranberries
2 oranges, quartered and seeded
4 T. liquid sweetener

Put cranberries and unpeeled oranges through coarse blade of food grinder. Stir in sweetener. Chill at least three hours before serving. Makes about 2 cups.

Darlene Kronschnabel

FROSTED CRANBERRIES

For a holiday touch around a mold or an entrée.

1 lb. washed and dried cranberries
1 egg white
Sugar

Beat egg white until frothy. Dip cranberries into egg white and then roll in sugar. Place on waxed paper to dry.

Naomi Arbit
June Turner

CRANBERRY-APPLE CIDER

1 lb. fresh or frozen cranberries
1 c. sweet cider
2 tart apples with skins, sliced
1 c. honey
Grated rind of 1 lemon
Pinch of ground mace

Simmer the cranberries, cider, and apples gently until fruit is soft. Add honey, rind, and mace. Simmer for 5 minutes. Cool. Serve with meat, fowl or fish. Makes 2 pints.

Darlene Kronschnabel

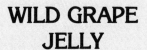

WILD GRAPE JELLY

FIRST DAY

Choose one beautiful, blue October day after the first light frost. Add a friend and drive out on your favorite country road. Watch the roadsides where the wild grapes flourish. Leisurely fill your baskets, stopping to enjoy the glory of autumn's coloring. Listen for the honking of wild geese and catch a glimpse of them in formation as they fly south. Pick a bunch of bittersweet to send to that faraway sister or friend. Return home early and set the table with fresh autumn leaves and vegetables from your own garden.

SECOND DAY

In the morning, cut the heavy stems from the grape bunches and pull out the thistle or milkweed down. Wash grapes, then follow this recipe:

Cover grapes with water. Bring to a boil and boil 20 minutes. Drain. Strain juice through jelly bag or thin cloth. To 6 cups of grape juice, add the strained juice of 1 lemon; heat to boiling. Add 1 package of powdered fruit pectin, bring to a boil, stir in 7½ cups of sugar. Bring to a rolling boil, boiling hard 1 minute, stirring constantly. Remove from heat; skim. Pour into jelly jars. Makes 6 half-pints.

Verna Sparks

Preserving Part of the Season

When beginning jelly and jam-making, use only tested recipes. The recipes must be followed exactly. Jelly, jams, and conserves are often compared to candy cookery. The problems are very similar: gel formation and prevention of crystallization. All ingredients must be measured accurately to prevent crystal formation. It is recommended to prepare only single recipes of jellies, jams, and conserves because it is a faster process and easier to control in small "batches." Essential equipment for jelly-making is a large, flat-bottomed kettle (8 to 10 quarts), a wooden spoon, and a clock with a second hand.

All ingredients in spreads have a very special purpose. For example, the fruit gives spreads its flavor and furnishes part of the pectin and acid which is needed for a successful gel. Pectin is the substance which causes the fruit juice to "jell." Without pectin, no fruit jelly is possible. Acid is needed for flavor and for the gel formation. If acid seems lacking, usually 1 tablespoon of strained lemon juice added to each standard measuring cup of fruit juice will supply the needed acid. Sugar is another vital ingredient. It is needed for gel formation, contributes flavor and serves as a preserving agent. Beet and cane sugar may be used with equal success.

Conserves are made from 2 or more fruits and have a jam-like consistency. A true conserve contains nuts. Jams are made by cooking crushed or chopped fruits with sugar until mixture rounds up in a spoon. Jelly is made by cooking fruit juice with sugar. The product should be firm enough to hold its shape when turned from the jar, yet soft enough to be spread with a knife.

There are two methods of testing for the jelly point—the sheet test and the temperature test. The sheet test is advised for the experienced cook. To use the sheet test, dip a cold metal spoon into the boiling jelly mixture. When 2 drops of jelly form together and sheet off the spoon, the jelly should be done. It is recommended to remove jellies, jams, and conserves from the cooking surface while testing for the jelly point. It is very easy to overcook a jelly or a jam. The temperature test is recommended for the inexperienced cook. It is probably the most dependable method for determining the jelly point. The jelly mixture is heated until the thermometer reaches the jelly point; then the kettle is removed from the heat immediately, and the jelly poured into hot sterilized jars. With the temperature test, it is vital that the thermometer is accurate.

Mary Lou Williamson

GRAPE AND PLUM JELLY

3 c. prepared juice (about 1½ lbs. fully ripe Concord grapes and 1½ lbs. fully ripe plums)
6 c. sugar
¾ c. water
1 1¾-oz. box powdered fruit pectin

To prepare the juice thoroughly crush grapes, one layer at a time. Place crushed fruit in jelly cloth or bag and squeeze out juice. Measure 1½ cups into large bowl or pan. Pit plums; do not peel. Chop very fine; then place in jelly cloth or bag and squeeze out enough juice to measure 1½ cups. Add to grape juice. Thoroughly mix sugar into juices. Mix water and fruit pectin in small saucepan. Bring to a boil and boil 1 minute, stirring constantly. Stir into the juices. Continue stirring about 3 minutes. (A few sugar crystals will remain.) Quickly pour into jars. Cover at once with tight lids. Let stand at room temperature until set, approximately 24 hours. Store in freezer. If jelly will be used within 2 or 3 weeks, it may be stored in refrigerator. Yields about 6 cups or 8 six-ounce glasses.

Note: For ease in extracting juice from grapes, heat fruit slightly; then crush using a potato masher or food mill.

PLUM RELISH

3½ c. prepared fruit (about 2 lbs. fully ripe plums)
¼ to 1 t. each cinnamon, cloves, allspice
½ c. vinegar
6½ c. sugar
½ bottle liquid fruit pectin

To prepare the fruit pit plums; do not peel. Chop very fine, and measure 3½ cups into a very large saucepan. Add spices and vinegar. Thoroughly mix sugar into fruit in saucepan. Place over high heat, bring to a full rolling boil and boil hard 1 minute, stirring constantly. Remove from heat and stir in fruit pectin immediately. Then stir and skim for 5 minutes to cool slightly and prevent floating fruit. Quickly ladle into glasses. Cover at once with ⅛ inch hot paraffin. Yields about 8 cups or about 10 six-ounce glasses.

APRICOT AND PLUM JAM

5 c. prepared fruit (about 2 lbs. fully ripe apricots and 1½ lbs. fully ripe plums)
7 c. sugar
1 1¾-oz. box powdered fruit pectin
¼ c. water

Prepare the fruit, pitting apricots and plums; do not peel. Cut into small pieces and grind or chop very fine. Measure 5 cups into a very large saucepan. Mix fruit pectin and water into fruit in saucepan. Place over high heat and stir until mixture comes to a hard boil. Add sugar. Bring to a full rolling boil and boil hard 1 minute, stirring constantly. Remove from heat and skim off foam with metal spoon. Then stir and skim for 5 minutes to cool slightly and to prevent floating fruit. Ladle quickly into glasses. Cover at once with ⅛ inch hot paraffin. Yields about 8¾ cups or 11 six-ounce glasses.

PEAR AND CRANBERRY JAM

3 c. prepared fruit (about 2 lbs. ripe Bartlett pears and 1 lb. cranberries)
1 t. grated orange rind
5 c. sugar
¾ c. water
1 1¾-oz. box powdered fruit pectin

Peel, core and finely chop pears. Measure 2 cups into a large bowl. Grind cranberries; measure 1 cup and add to pears. Stir in orange rind; add sugar. Mix well and let stand. Mix water and pectin in small saucepan; bring to boil and boil 1 minute, stirring constantly. Stir into fruit mixture. Continue stirring about 3 minutes. (There will be a few remaining sugar crystals.) Quickly ladle into glasses. Cover at once with tight lids. When jam is set (approximately 24 hours) store in freezer. Jam may be stored in refrigerator if used within 2 to 3 weeks. Yields about 7 medium size glasses.

Fruits for the Freezer

Thaw frozen fruits in the unopened package, either in the refrigerator, at room temperature, in front of a fan, or in a pan of cool water.

PLUMS

Select firm, ripe fruit, soft enough to yield to slight pressure. Wash, halve and pit. Prepare in one of the following ways:

Syrup Pack: Prepare 50 per cent syrup. Pack the fruit in freezer jar or plastic freezer box. Cover with syrup, leaving head space. Seal, label, and freeze.

Sugar Pack: Mix five parts fruit with one part sugar. Allow to set until sugar is dissolved. Pack in freezer jar or plastic freezer box, leaving head space. Seal, label, and freeze.

PEARS

Select full-flavored pears that are crisp and firm, not mealy in texture. Wash, peel, core, and drop into ascorbic acid—citric acid mixture. Leave in halves or cut in quarters or slice. Prepare a 40 per cent syrup and boil. Blanch drained pears 2 minutes, cool and pack in freezer jar or plastic freezer box, leaving head space. Cover with cool syrup. Seal, label, and freeze.

To make a 40 per cent syrup, dissolve 3 cups sugar in 4 cups water until clear.

APPLESAUCE

Wash apples, peel if desired, core, and slice. To each quart of apples, add 1/3 cup water and ¼ teaspoon ascorbic acid. Cook apples until tender, puree, and add ¼ cup sugar to one quart of hot puree, stirring until dissolved. Cool and package in freezer jars or plastic freezer boxes, leaving head space. Seal, label, and freeze.

How to Can Autumn Fruits

To keep fruit from darkening, use ascorbic acid and citric acid mixtures according to manufacturer's instructions.

Since iron causes many fruits to darken, knives, mixing bowls, pans and other containers should be of stainless steel or other non-corrosive material.

APPLES

Make light or medium syrup. Wash, drain, core, pare, and slice cooking apples (or cut into halves or quarters). Treat to prevent darkening. Drain. Boil in syrup 5 minutes. Pack, hot, into hot mason jars, leaving ½-inch head space. Cover with boiling syrup, leaving ½-inch head space. Adjust caps. Process pints and quarts 20 minutes in boiling-water bath.

APPLES

Select full-flavored apples that are crisp and firm, not mealy in texture. Wash, peel, and core. Slice medium apples into twelfths, larger ones into sixteenths. Drop immediately into ascorbic acid—citric acid water.

Syrup Pack: Use 50 per cent syrup and add ½ teaspoon ascorbic acid to each quart of syrup. Pour ½ cup cold syrup into a freezer jar or plastic freezer box. Press apple slices down in container and add enough syrup to cover, leaving head space. Seal, label, and freeze.

To make a 50 per cent syrup, dissolve 4¾ cups sugar in 4 cups lukewarm water until clear.

SWEET CHERRIES

Select bright, fully ripened cherries of dark colored varieties. Wash, stem, and pit. To retain the natural fruit flavor, add ½ teaspoon ascorbic acid to 1 quart of the 50 per cent syrup. Package the same as berries (syrup pack).

APPLESAUCE

Wash, pare (if desired), quarter, and core cooking apples. Simmer, covered, in a small amount of water until tender. Press apples through sieve or food mill. Sweeten sauce to taste (about ¼ cup sugar to 4 medium apples). Reheat to boiling. Pour, boiling hot, into hot mason jars, leaving ½-inch head space. Stir with rubber bottle scraper to similar non-metal utensil to remove air bubbles. Adjust caps. Process pints and quarts 20 minutes in boiling-water bath.

PEACHES

Make medium or heavy syrup. Wash and scald peaches. Cut into halves, pit and peel. Treat to prevent darkening. Drain. Cook a few peaches at a time in syrup until hot through. Pack, hot, into hot mason jars, leaving ½-inch head space. Cover with boiling syrup, leaving ½-inch head space. Adjust caps. Process pints 20 minutes, quarts 25 minutes, in boiling-water bath.

PLUMS

Plums may be scalded and peeled, but are usually canned unpeeled. Prick plums with needle. Pricking does not prevent skins from cracking, but helps prevent the fruit from bursting. Make medium or heavy syrup. Wash and drain plums. Heat syrup to boiling. Add plums (not more than 2 layers in pan). Remove pan from heat 2 minutes after adding fruit. Cover. Let stand 20 to 30 minutes. Pack plums into hot mason jars, leaving ½-inch head space. Reheat syrup to boiling. Pour over plums, leaving ½-inch head space. Adjust caps. Process pints 20 minutes, quarts 25 minutes, in boiling-water bath.

APRICOTS

Tree-ripened apricots may be canned whole. Pits should be removed from fruit harvested before it was fully ripe. Some varieties of apricots should be packed raw because they do not hold their shape when heated before packing.

Make medium or heavy syrup. Wash and scald apricots. Remove pits and skins. Treat to prevent darkening. Drain. Cook a few apricots at a time in syrup until hot through. Pack, hot, into hot mason jars, leaving ½-inch head space. Adjust caps. Process pints 20 minutes, quarts 25 minutes, in boiling-water bath.

Preserving Vegetables

Home canning is a highly rewarding experience . . . It can be economical, creative, and personally satisfying. When the jars of fresh fruits and vegetables you have "put up" during the season are all lined up on the shelf, you have meal after meal all ready to heat, or chill, and serve. The foods are there, at your fingertips, to feed your family and friends and to give as gifts to very special people. For canning efficiency and enjoyment, here are some helpful hints.

Start planning several weeks in advance of the canning season. Make a list of the kinds and amounts of canned food you need and want in the months ahead.

Decide the sizes and types of jars you are going to need.

Check your steam pressure and water-bath canners to be sure they are in perfect condition. Low acid vegetables such as asparagus, beans, corn, okra, pumpkin and spinach must be processed in a steam-pressure canner at a temperature of 240°. Fruits and acid vegetables such as rhubarb, sauerkraut and tomatoes must be processed in a water-bath canner at a temperature of 212°.

It's more enjoyable if you process a few jars every morning for a number of days rather than devote a whole day to canning. Can vegetables when they are garden-fresh and at the best stage for cooking.

Wash, drain, and prepare only enough produce for a canner load. Process by the recommended method and for the correct amount of time for the specific food being canned.

Set jars upright, far apart, and out of a draft to cool. Remove bands about 24 hours after canning.

Store jars—without bands—in a dark, cool, dry area.

Home canned foods will keep for many years.

Some foods hold color, flavor, texture and food value longer than others. The cooler the storage space, the longer the canned food will retain its freshly cooked color and flavor.

A FROZEN THOUGHT OR TWO

With gardens "in" and vegetables slowly beginning to sprout, many homemakers are wondering—should I can or should I freeze. Freezing within the past few years has become a first-rate method for preserving many of our fresh foods. The popularity of frozen food is here to stay and is gaining favor with homemakers because of the food quality, ease in processing and most important today—economic assistance with the shrinking food dollar.

Many homemakers may have a thought or two about freezing vegetables. Do not hesitate a minute; vegetables such as snap beans, corn, tomatoes, carrots, and broccoli can be frozen and prepared in such tasty dishes that your family will yearn for more. The secret to "good freezing" is planting the proper variety for freezing, picking the vegetables at the correct stage of maturity (not underripe or overripe), correct blanching time, cooling by immersing in ice water and the immediate placement of the packaged food in the quick-freeze of the freezer.

If the proper freezing methods are followed, the frozen food will be high in food value and will show little change in color, flavor and texture.

Most vegetables can be cooked without thawing. The exception is corn on the cob, which should be completely thawed before being cooked. All greens should be partially thawed so as to separate them before cooking.

Mary Lou Williamson

CAULIFLOWER

Choose compact heads. Trim, break into flowerets of uniform size, about 1 inch across. Wash carefully and drain. Prepare and package same as broccoli.

GARDEN PEAS

Harvest when pods are filled with young tender peas that have not become starchy. Wash, shell, wash, scald 2 minutes. Cool, drain, and package in plastic freezer bag, jar, or plastic freezer box. Seal, label, and freeze.

TOMATOES

Wash and drain enough fresh, firm, red-ripe tomatoes for 1 canner load. Put tomatoes in a wire basket or cheesecloth. Place in boiling water about ½ minute to loosen skins. Dip into cold water. Drain. Cut out all cores, remove skins and trim off any green spots. Cut tomatoes in quarters or leave whole. Pack tomatoes into hot mason jars, pressing tomatoes until spaces fill with juice, leaving ½-inch head space. Add 1 teaspoon salt to each quart if desired. Adjust caps. Process pints 35 minutes, quarts 45 minutes, in boiling-water bath.

GREEN PEAS

Wash, drain, and shell freshly gathered peas. Wash again. Boil small peas 3 minutes; larger ones 5 minutes. Pour, hot, into hot mason jars, leaving 1-inch head space. Add 1 teaspoon salt to each quart. Add boiling water, if needed, to cover, leaving 1-inch head space. Adjust caps. Process pints and quarts 40 minutes at 10 pounds pressure. If peas are extra large, process 10 minutes longer.

OKRA

Use young, tender okra. If to be added to soup, it should be sliced; otherwise can pods whole. Wash and drain okra. Remove stem and blossom ends without cutting into pod. Boil 2 minutes. Pack, hot, into hot mason jars, leaving 1-inch head space. Add 1 teaspoon salt to each quart. If needed, add boiling water to cover, leaving 1-inch head space. Adjust caps. Process pints 25 minutes, quarts 40 minutes, at 10 pounds pressure.

GREEN, SNAP, AND WAX BEANS

Wash, drain, string, trim ends, and break or cut freshly gathered beans into 2-inch pieces. Boil 3 minutes. Pack, hot, into hot mason jars, leaving 1-inch head space. Add 1 teaspoon salt to each quart. Cover with boiling water, leaving 1-inch head space. Adjust caps. Process pints 20 minutes, quarts 25 minutes, at 10 pounds pressure.

Note: The processing time given applies only to young, tender pods. Beans that have almost reached the "shell-out" stage require 15 to 20 minutes longer processing time.

BROCCOLI

Select firm, young, tender stalks with compact heads. Wash and remove leaves and woody portions. Separate heads into convenient-size sections and immerse in brine (1 c. salt to 1 gal. water) for 30 minutes. Rinse and drain. Scald medium-size sections 3 minutes and large-size sections 4 minutes. Cool, drain and package in plastic freezer bag, jar, or plastic freezer box. Seal, label and freeze.

CORN ON THE COB

Select only the tender, freshly gathered corn which is in the milk stage. If a kernel of corn is pinched and a milky substance oozes forth, this is described as the "milk stage." Husk and trim the ears, remove the silks and wash the corn.

To freeze corn for corn on the cob, scald the ears of corn which are 1½ inches in diameter for 6 minutes; ears 2 inches in diameter should be scalded 8 minutes and the larger ears of corn scalded 10 minutes. Cool the scalded ears of corn thoroughly and drain. Each ear of corn should be wrapped individually in moisture-vapor-proof film. Next, place each film-wrapped ear of corn in a plastic freezer bag and seal immediately. Label your corn on the cob with name of the product and date frozen. Place the corn in the quick-freeze compartment of the freezer. Completely thaw before cooking.

WHOLE TOMATOES

Wash and drain only enough tomatoes for 6 freezer containers. Place the tomatoes in a wire basket or cheesecloth. Place tomatoes in boiling water about ½ minute to loosen the skins. Next, dip the tomatoes into cold water and drain. Cut out all cores, remove skins and trim off any green spots. The tomatoes are left whole and packed into rigid containers or freezing jars. No head space is needed in the containers because of the space for expansion around the whole tomatoes. The frozen tomatoes can be easily substituted for canned tomatoes in recipes. Do not forget to seal the containers, label and immediately place in the freezer.

TOMATOES WITH OKRA

Use equal measure of sliced okra and peeled, cored, and chopped tomatoes. Cook tomatoes 20 minutes. Add okra. Boil 5 minutes. Pour, hot, into hot mason jars, leaving 1-inch head space. Add 1 teaspoon salt to each quart. Adjust caps. Process pints 30 minutes, quarts 35 minutes, at 10 pounds pressure. 1 small onion may be chopped and added to each quart of tomatoes before cooking.

ASPARAGUS

Wash and drain tender, tight-tipped asparagus. Remove tough ends and scales. Wash again. Leave asparagus whole or cut into 1-inch pieces. Boil 3 minutes. Pack, hot, into hot mason jars, leaving 1-inch head space. Add 1 teaspoon salt to each quart. Cover with boiling water, leaving 1-inch head space. Adjust caps. Process pints 25 minutes, quarts 30 minutes, at 10 pounds pressure.

WHOLE KERNEL CORN

Husk corn; remove silk. Wash. Cut corn from cob. Do not scrape. Measure. Add 1 teaspoon salt and 2 cups boiling water to each quart of corn. Pack, boiling hot, into hot mason jars, leaving 1-inch head space. Adjust caps. Process pints 55 minutes, quarts 1 hour and 25 minutes, at 10 pounds pressure.

CARROTS

Wash and scrape carrots. Wash again. Slice, dice or leave whole. Boil 3 minutes. Pack, hot, into hot mason jars, leaving 1-inch head space. Add 1 teaspoon salt to each quart. Cover with boiling water, leaving 1-inch head space. Adjust caps. Process pints 25 minutes, quarts 30 minutes, at 10 pounds pressure.

PUMPKIN

Wash firm, fully ripe pumpkin. Cut into large pieces. Discard seeds. Steam or bake until tender. Scoop out pulp. Put through sieve or food mill. Add boiling water to make pulp a little thinner than needed for pies. Pour, hot, into hot mason jars, leaving 1-inch head space. Add 1 teaspoon salt to each quart. Adjust caps. Process pints 1 hour and 5 minutes, quarts 1 hour and 20 minutes, at 10 pounds pressure.

Pickles and Relishes

Did you ever realize you don't need to pickle a pickle? Why not try okra, peppers, crab apples, or even zucchini pickles—they are super as pickled products.

How about some pickling hints for a successful pickling venture. Premium pickle products cannot be obtained unless top quality ingredients are selected. Check the fruits or vegetables for pickling; they should be unwaxed. The pickling brine cannot penetrate a waxed vegetable. The best salt for preparing a brine is a pure granulated salt. Uniodized salt will produce a cloudy brine while iodized salt may cause the pickles to darken. The best vinegar for pickling is either cider or distilled, but read the label before purchasing. A vinegar for pickling should have an acidity of 4 to 6 percent if a firm pickled product is desired. A word of caution—if a crisp pickled product is desired, DO NOT DILUTE the vinegar unless stated in the recipe. Fresh spices are recommended for the best flavored products. Spices deteriorate quickly in heat and humidity. Alum and lime are not needed to make pickles crisp and firm if good quality ingredients and up-to-date procedures are used.

Today, all pickle products require heat treatment to destroy organisms that cause spoilage and to inactivate enzymes that may affect flavor, color and texture. Adequate heating is best achieved by processing the filled jars in a boiling-water bath. Check the water level in the water bath—it should be 2 inches over the jar tops. Count the processing time when the water begins to boil. The end result will be a delicate pickled product when the lush green gardens are gone.

Mary Lou Williamson

END-OF-SUMMER RELISH

Vary this vegetable combination to suit your taste and the contents of your vegetable crisper.

2 c. sliced cauliflower flowerets (about ½ small head)
2 carrots, julienne strips
1 green pepper, cut in strips
10 to 12 green beans
1 zucchini, cut in disks
1 small jar stuffed olives
¾ c. wine vinegar
¼ c. olive oil

1 T. sugar
1 t. salt
½ t. oregano
¼ t. pepper
¼ c. water
Cherry tomatoes

Combine all ingredients in a large pan. Bring to a boil and simmer, covered, 5 minutes. Cool and let marinate at least 24 hours. Cherry tomatoes may be added just before serving. Makes 2½ quarts.

Naomi Arbit
June Turner

END-OF-THE-GARDEN PICKLES

1 c. sliced cucumbers
1 c. chopped sweet peppers
1 c. chopped cabbage
1 c. sliced onions
1 c. chopped green tomatoes
1 c. chopped carrots
1 c. green beans, cut in 1-inch pieces

1 c. chopped celery
2 T. mustard seed
1 T. celery seed
2 c. cider vinegar
2 c. sugar
2 T. turmeric

Combine cucumbers, peppers, cabbage, onions, and tomatoes in large container. Soak in salt brine (½ cup salt to 2 quarts cold water) overnight. Drain well. Combine and cook the carrots and green beans until tender. Drain well. Mix all vegetables together with remaining ingredients. Boil 10 minutes. Pack into hot, sterilized jars. Adjust caps. Process 10 minutes in boiling-water bath. Makes about 6 pints.

Darlene Kronschnabel

ZUCCHINI PICKLES

2 lbs. fresh, firm zucchini
2 small (or medium) onions
¼ c. salt (pickling salt is best)
2 c. white sugar
3 c. cider vinegar (4 to 6 percent acid strength)

1 t. celery salt
1 t. turmeric
2 t. mustard seed

Wash zucchini and cut in thin slices. Peel and cut onions in quarters, then slice very thin. Add to zucchini. Cover zucchini and onions with an inch of water and add salt. Let stand 2 hours. Drain thoroughly.

Bring remaining ingredients to boiling. Pour over zucchini and onions. Let stand 2 hours. Bring all ingredients to boiling point and heat 5 minutes.

Pack into preheated jars. Leave ⅛-inch head space. Adjust caps and process in water-bath canner at simmering temperature for 15 minutes. Cool. Test for seal. Store.

CORN RELISH

8 c. corn, boiled and cut from cob
4 c. chopped cabbage
1 c. chopped sweet green pepper
1 c. chopped sweet red pepper
2 large onions, chopped
1 c. sugar

2 T. ground mustard
1 T. mustard seed
1 T. salt
1 T. celery seed
4 c. cider vinegar
1 c. water

Combine all ingredients in large, heavy kettle. Simmer 20 minutes. You may add more sugar and salt to taste. Pack, boiling hot, into sterilized jars, leaving ½-inch headspace. Adjust caps. Process 10 minutes in boiling-water bath. Makes about 6 pints.

Darlene Kronschnabel

The Golden Breads of Autumn

SWEET POTATO BREAD

2 c. flour
⅓ c. sugar
⅓ c. dark brown sugar, firmly packed
1 T. baking powder
1 t. salt
¼ t. ground allspice
2 eggs, beaten
1 c. mashed cooked sweet potato
½ c. milk
3 T. vegetable oil
½ c. chopped pecans
6 pecans halves (optional)
1 egg white, beaten (optional)

Stir together flour, sugars, baking powder, salt, and allspice. Blend together eggs, sweet potato, milk, and oil. Stir in chopped pecans, then add all at once to flour mixture, stirring until blended. Pour into greased 4½ x 8½-inch loaf pan. Bake in a 350° oven 1 hour and 10 minutes. If desired, dip pecan halves into beaten egg white and place on top of loaf for last 10 minutes of baking. Cool on wire rack 10 minutes before removing from pan; cool completely before slicing. Makes 1 loaf.

Darlene Kronschnabel

ZUCCHINI-BRAN BREAD

¼ c. soy flour
2 T. nutritional yeast
1½ c. bran
2⅔ c. whole wheat flour
1 T. baking powder
½ t. baking soda
1 t. salt
1½ t. cinnamon
¼ t. ginger
¾ c. honey
⅓ c. vegetable oil
½ c. milk
2 eggs, beaten
2 c. grated zucchini
¼ c. chopped nuts
½ c. raisins

Preheat oven to 325°. Stir first 9 dry ingredients together. In a separate bowl, stir together honey, oil, milk, and eggs. Add honey mixture to dry ingredients; stir in zucchini, nuts, and raisins. Pour into well-greased 9 x 5-inch loaf pan or two 7 x 4-inch pans and bake 60 minutes or until golden (less time for smaller loaves). Cool 10 minutes in pan and then turn out onto wire racks to finish cooling. Makes one 9 x 5-inch loaf or two 7 x 4-inch loaves.

Donna M. Paananen

PUMPKIN BREAD

¾ c. margarine or shortening
2¼ c. brown sugar, firmly packed
4 eggs

2 c. cooked pumpkin purée
⅔ c. water
3¾ c. whole wheat flour
1 T. nutritional yeast
2 T. soy flour
½ t. baking powder
2 t. baking soda
1 t. salt
1¼ t. cinnamon
1¼ t. ground cloves
⅔ c. regular or golden raisins or chopped dates
⅔ c. chopped nuts

Preheat oven to 350°. In a large mixing bowl, cream shortening and sugar thoroughly; add eggs and beat until light. Stir in pumpkin and water. In a separate bowl, stir together the flour, nutritional yeast, soy flour, baking powder, soda, salt, and spices. Stir dry ingredients into pumpkin mixture. Finally fold in nuts and raisins. Pour into 3 well-greased 9 x 5 x 3-inch loaf pans or 1-pound coffee cans. Bake for 1 hour or until done (toothpick inserted in center comes out clean). Let cool 10 minutes before removing from pans to finish cooling on wire racks. Tastes better the second day. Makes 3 loaves.

Donna M. Paananen

SWEET CORN BREAD

1 c. coarsely ground cornmeal
2 c. white flour
1 T. baking powder
½ t. salt
1½ c. sugar
4 large eggs, separated
1 c. milk or half-and-half
1 t. vanilla extract
¾ c. melted butter

Combine the cornmeal, flour, baking powder, salt, and sugar. Combine the egg yolks, milk, vanilla, and melted butter. Stir

into the dry ingredients until they are thoroughly moistened. Beat the egg whites until stiff and fold into the batter carefully. Pour into a 3-quart shallow baking pan that has been buttered well. Bake in a 350° oven for 30 minutes, or until it tests done. If desired, 2 8-inch square pans may be used.

Darlene Kronschnabel

APPLE BREAD

½ c. margarine
½ c. honey
¼ c. old-fashioned molasses
2 eggs
2 t. baking powder
½ t. salt
1⅔ c. whole wheat flour
⅓ c. non-instant powdered milk
⅔ c. raw wheat germ
2 c. chopped, peeled apples
⅔ c. broken nuts

TOPPING

4 T. melted margarine
5 T. whole wheat flour
1 T. wheat germ
4 T. brown sugar, well packed
2 t. cinnamon

Preheat oven to 350°. Mix together thoroughly the first four ingredients. Stir dry ingredients together and combine with wet, blending well. Stir in apples until well blended and add nuts. Pour into well-greased bread pan. Mix topping together with a fork and sprinkle evenly over batter. Bake for one hour or until top springs back when pressed lightly.

Donna M. Paananen

CRANBERRY-ORANGE BREAD

1¾ c. whole wheat flour
¼ c. wheat germ
2 T. soy flour
¾ c. brown sugar
1½ t. baking powder
½ t. baking soda
2 T. melted margarine, cooled slightly
    Grated rind and juice of 1 orange plus water or more orange juice to make ¾ c.
1 egg, beaten
1 c. raw cranberries, cut in halves

Preheat oven to 350°. In a large bowl, blend dry ingredients. Mix in margarine, orange mixture, and egg. Fold in cranberries. Pour into well-greased 9 x 5 x 3-inch loaf pan. Bake 45 to 60 minutes or until top springs back when touched lightly and bread pulls away slightly from sides of pan. Cool about 10 minutes before removing from pan. Cool on wire rack. (Bread is better the second day.) Makes 1 loaf.

Donna M. Paananen

Thanksgiving Pies

PUMPKIN CHEESE PIE

1 8-oz. pkg. cream cheese, softened
¾ c. sugar
1 t. cinnamon   3 eggs
½ t. cloves   1 16-oz. can pumpkin
½ t. ginger   1 t. vanilla
½ t. nutmeg   Pecan halves (optional)
½ t. salt   1 9-inch pie crust, unbaked

Beat cream cheese until fluffy, gradually adding sugar combined with spices. Add eggs one at a time, beating well after each. Beat in pumpkin and vanilla. Pour into prepared shell. Bake in a preheated 350° oven for 40 minutes or until knife inserted in center comes out clean. During last 15 minutes of baking, pecan halves may be placed on top as decoration. Chill before serving. Serves 8 to 10.

Naomi Arbit
June Turner

GOLDEN APPLE-PECAN PIE

2 Golden Delicious apples, peeled and sliced
3 eggs
¾ c. brown sugar
⅛ t. salt
¾ c. light corn syrup
2 t. butter
⅔ c. coarsely chopped pecans
  Pastry for single-crust pie

Line a 9-inch pie plate with pastry. Place apple slices in bottom of pie plate. Beat eggs; add remaining ingredients, reserving a few pecan halves or large pieces, and mix well. Bake in a 425° oven for 10 minutes. Then reduce heat to 300° and bake for about one hour or until set. Garnish with whipped cream and a few pecan halves.

Darlene Kronschnabel

HOMEMADE MINCEMEAT

½ lb. fresh beef suet, chopped fine
4 c. seedless raisins
2 c. dried currants
1¼ c. chopped candied fruit
½ c. chopped dried figs
4 c. chopped, peeled cored apples
1 c. coarsely chopped nuts
1¼ c. sugar
1 t. ground nutmeg
1 t. ground allspice
1 t. ground cinnamon
½ t. ground cloves
2½ c. brandy
1 c. dry red wine

Combine the suet, fruit, nuts, sugar, and spices in a large mixing bowl and stir together thoroughly. Pour in the brandy and wine, and mix with a large wooden spoon until all ingredients are well moistened. Cover the bowl and set the mincemeat aside in a cool place (not in the refrigerator) for at least three weeks.

Check the mincemeat once a week. As the liquid is absorbed by the fruit, replenish it with wine and brandy, using about ¼ cup of each at a time. Mincemeat can be kept indefinitely in a covered container in the refrigerator. Makes 3 quarts.

To make pies with homemade mincemeat, prepare your favorite pastry for a two-crust pie. Line the pan with the bottom crust. Add undrained mincemeat. Add top crust. Bake in a 425° oven 30 minutes or until done.

OLD-FASHIONED MINCEMEAT PIE

3 c. prepared mincemeat
1½ c. coarsely broken walnuts
½ c. brown sugar, packed
½ c. brandy
  Pastry for two-crust, 9-inch pie
4 T. butter, softened
1 T. light cream

Combine walnuts, mincemeat, brown sugar, and brandy; refrigerate to allow flavors to mingle. You can do this for several days. Roll out pastry for bottom crust, spread with two tablespoons butter; fold into thirds; refrigerate until well chilled; repeat with top crust. Heat oven to 425°. Roll out pastry crust. Fill with undrained mincemeat mixture. Adjust top crust; brush top with light cream. Bake 30 minutes or until nicely browned.

Darlene Kronschnabel

Halloween Magic

When dry leaves rattle in the wind
And sheaves of wheat stand tall,
And high within October's skies
One hears the blackbirds call;
When Indian corn is harvested
And peanuts freshly dug,
And sweet potatoes laid to dry
Upon the old hooked rug.

When cords of wood stand ready
For winter days ahead,
And all the feather mattresses
Are put back on the beds;
When black iron stoves hum merrily
Till long into the night,
And mince pies in the oven
Bring sighs of pure delight.

When round-eyed children breathlessly
Admire Dad's matchless skill
In carving jack-o'-lanterns
For every windowsill,
And with her sharpest scissors
Mother makes the most
Of old discarded linens
To dress each little ghost!

When lamplight casts long shadows
About the quiet rooms,
And Grandma tells of witches
That ride upon their brooms;
Imagination quickens
As branches brush the screen,
For there's an age-old magic
In the night of Halloween!

Grace E. Easley

For This Is Halloween

Without a sound, spooks prowl around,
    For this is Halloween.
The white ghosts bound upon the ground,
    For this is Halloween.
The shadows gaunt, their long arms flaunt,
But ghouls and goblins never daunt.
Across the sky the queer shades fly,
    For this is Halloween.

Strange Jack-o-lights shine in the night,
    For this is Halloween.
Each eerie sprite shrinks from the sight,
    For this is Halloween.
The night-winds groan and shriek and moan,
And children mustn't be alone,
While black cats race, and fairies chase,
    For this is Halloween.

The owls dart and make one start,
    For this is Halloween.
With subtle art, elves play their part,
    For this is Halloween.
Like omens ill, the dead leaves fill
Each doorway and each windowsill;
When pumpkins glow, then we all know,
    This must be Halloween.

Hazel Adell Jackson

Night of Enchantment

When Autumn creeps up the hillsides
On silent frost-shod feet,
Following in its footsteps
Is the night when goblins meet.

'Tis on this night Fall weaves a spell
Round folks both young and old,
And strange enchantment fills the air
As witching hours unfold.

Up in the moon, old Pumpkin Face
Emits an eerie light,
And yowling cats arch high their spines,
As howling dogs take flight.

Cackling witches take o'er the sky
On broomstick aeroplanes,

While bats suspended, wrong side up,
Watch from the weather vanes.

Weird little forms, strangely attired,
Dance up and down the street,
Leaving behind when they depart,
Echoes of "Trick or Treat."

Jack-o'-lanterns with pixie smiles
Seem to enjoy the fun,
But screeching owls appear to say
They'll gladly see it done.

Witches, goblins, and spooks galore
Choose this night to convene,
And none but brave folk dare go out
The eve of Halloween.

Inez Marrs

When the Frost
Is on the Punkin

When the frost is on the punkin and the fodder's in the shock,
And you hear the kyouck and gobble of the struttin' turkeycock,
And the clackin' of the guineys, and the cluckin' of the hens,
And the rooster's hallylooyer as he tiptoes on the fence;
O it's then's the times a feller is a feelin' at his best,
With the risin' sun to greet him from a night of peaceful rest,
As he leaves the house, bareheaded, and goes out to feed the stock,
When the frost is on the punkin and the fodder's in the shock.

They's something kindo' harty-like about the atmusfere
When the heat of summer's over and the coolin' fall is here—
Of course we miss the flowers, and the blossoms on the trees,
And the mumble of the hummin'-birds and buzzin' of the bees;
But the air's so appetizin'; and the landscape through the haze
Of a crisp and sunny mornin' of the airly autumn days
Is a pictur' that no painter has the colorin' to mock—
When the frost is on the punkin and the fodder's in the shock.

The husky, rusty russel of the tossels of the corn,
And the raspin' of the tangled leaves, as golden as the morn;
The stubble in the furries—kindo' lonesome-like, but still
A-preachin' sermuns to us of the barns they growed to fill;
The strawstack in the medder, and the reaper in the shed;
The hosses in theyr stalls below—the clover overhead!
O it sets my hart a-clickin' like the tickin' of a clock,
When the frost is on the punkin and the fodder's in the shock.

Then your apples all is getherd, and the ones a feller keeps
Is poured around the celler-floor in red and yeller heaps;
And your cider-makin's over, and your wimmern-folks is through
With their mince and apple-butter, and theyr souse and sausage, too! . . .
I don't know how to tell it—but ef sich a thing could be
As the angels wantin' boardin', and they'd call around on me—
I'd want to 'commodate 'em— all the whole-indurin' flock—
When the frost is on the punkin and the fodder's in the shock.

James Whitcomb Riley

The Pumpkin

Ah! On Thanksgiving Day, when from east and from west
From north and from south come the pilgrim and guest,
When the gray-haired New England sees round his board
The old broken links of affection restored,
When the care-wearied man seeks his mother once more,
And the worn matron smiles where the girl smiled before,
What moistens the lip and what brightens the eye?
What calls back the past like the rich pumpkin pie?

Oh—fruit loved of boyhood—the old days recalling,
When woodgrapes were purpling and brown nuts were falling!
When wild, ugly faces we carved in its skin,
Glaring out through the dark with a candle within!
When we laughed round the corn-heap, with hearts all in tune
Our chair a broad pumpkin, our lantern the moon,
Telling tales of a fairy who travelled like steam,
In a pumpkin-shell coach, with two rats for her team!

John Greenleaf Whittier

44

TOASTED PUMPKIN SEEDS

Take 2 cups pumpkin seeds, washed and drained. Spread seeds on a cookie sheet, sprinkle with salt. Toast in a 350° oven for 15 minutes.

PUMPKIN BUTTER

3½ c. cooked pumpkin (1 29-oz. can)
4½ c. sugar
  1 T. pumpkin pie spice
  1 1¾-oz. box powdered fruit pectin

To make the butter, measure 3½ cups pumpkin into a large saucepan. Measure sugar and set aside. Add spice and fruit pectin to the pumpkin and mix well. Place over high heat and stir until mixture comes to a hard boil. Add all sugar immediately and stir. Bring to a full rolling boil and boil hard 1 minute, stirring constantly. Remove from heat. Ladle quickly into glasses. Cover at once with ⅛ inch hot paraffin. Yields about 5½ cups or 7 six-ounce glasses.

PUMPKIN CAKE

  1 c. unbleached white flour
  2 c. whole wheat flour
¼ c. wheat germ
  2 t. baking powder
  2 t. baking soda
  2 t. cinnamon
  1 t. freshly ground nutmeg
  1 t. salt
  2 c. brown sugar, firmly packed
1¼ c. vegetable oil
1⅓ c. pumpkin purée, fresh or canned
  4 eggs
¾ c. seedless raisins
¾ c. golden raisins
1½ c. chopped walnuts, pecans, or other nuts

Preheat oven to 350°. Mix together the first 8 dry ingredients. Set aside. Place the sugar, oil, and pumpkin purée in a large mixing bowl and beat well at medium speed. Add the eggs, one at a time, beating well after each addition. Fold dry ingredients into the wet ingredients. Finally, stir in raisins and nuts. Pour into a well-greased 10-inch bundt or tube pan. Bake 1¼ hours or until done. Cake will be brown in color. Let cool 10 minutes in pan before turning out onto a rack. Can be frozen very successfully at this point. When serving, sprinkle with confectioners' sugar and, if desired, ground nuts. Makes 16 to 24 slices.

Donna M. Paananen

Pumpkins are as much a part of our American heritage as Betsy Ross. No doubt our forefathers served pumpkins, or "pumpions" as they were called, at their first Thanksgiving feast.

The pumpkin sustained the Pilgrims for many years. Easy to grow, it offered fruit for the table and for the animals. Pilgrims used pumpkins for pies, puddings, and custards, and served them at any meal.

The First Thanksgiving

Our harvest being gotten in, our Governor sente four men out fowling that so we might, after a more special manner, rejoyce together after we had gathered the fruit of our labours. These four, in one day, killed as much fowl as, with a little help besides, served the company almost a week, at which time, amongst other recreations, we exercised our armes, many of the Indians coming amongst us.

And amongst the rest, their greatest King, Massasoit, with some ninety men, whom, for three days, we entertained and feasted.

And they went out and killed five deer, which they brought to the Plantation, and bestowed on our Governor and upon the Captaine and others.

And although it be not always so plentiful as it was at this time with us, yet, by the goodness of God, we are so farr from wante that we often wish you partakers of our plentie.

Edward Winslow
Plymouth, Massachusetts, 1621
A Letter to England

The First Thanksgiving

Indian summer soon came in a blaze of glory, and it was time to bring in the crops. All in all, their first harvest was a disappointment. Their twenty acres of corn, thanks to Squanto, had done well enough. But the Pilgrims failed miserably with the more familiar crops. Still, it was possible to make a substantial increase in the individual weekly food ration which for months had consisted merely of a peck of meal from the stores brought on the *Mayflower*. This was doubled by adding a peck of maize a week, and the company decreed a holiday so that all might, "after a more special manner, rejoyce together."

The Pilgrims had other things to be thankful for. They had made peace with the Indians and walked "as peaceably and safely in the woods as in the highways of England." A start had been made in the beaver trade. There had been no sickness for months. Eleven houses now lined the street—seven private dwellings and four buildings for common use. There had been no recurrence of mutiny and dissension. Faced with common dangers, saints and strangers had drawn closer together, sinking doctrinal differences for a time. . . .

As the day of the harvest approached, four men were sent out to shoot waterfowl, returning with enough to supply the company for a week. Massasoit was invited to attend and shortly arrived—with ninety ravenous braves! The strain on the larder was somewhat eased when some of these went out and bagged five deer. Captain Standish staged a military review

GARDEN HARVEST CASSEROLE

1 c. sliced and unpeeled eggplant	
1 c. thinly sliced carrots	3 cloves garlic, crushed
1 c. sliced green beans	3 sprigs parsley, chopped
1 c. diced potatoes	Freshly ground black
2 medium tomatoes, quartered	pepper
1 small yellow squash, sliced	1 c. beef bouillon
1 small zucchini, sliced	⅓ c. vegetable oil
1 medium onion, sliced	2 t. salt
½ c. chopped green pepper	¼ t. tarragon
½ c. chopped cabbage	½ bay leaf, crumpled

Mix vegetables together and place into a shallow baking dish (13 x 9 x 2-inch). Sprinkle parsley and grind pepper over all. At this point you can refrigerate until ready to bake. Preheat oven to 350°. Pour bouillon into a small saucepan; add oil, salt, tarragon, and bay leaf. Heat to boiling; correct seasonings. Pour over vegetables. Cover baking dish with aluminum foil; bake 1 to 1½ hours or until vegetables are just tender and are still colorful. Carefully stir vegetables occasionally; but to preserve color, don't lift cover off for very long. Serves 6 to 8.

Note: You can substitute other vegetables if they are in harvest and they appeal to you.

Donna M. Paananen

MUSHROOM & WILD RICE STUFFING

½ c. butter	⅔ c. water
1 lb. fresh mushrooms, sliced	4 c. cooked wild rice
½ c. chopped onions	1½ t. salt
½ c. minced parsley	⅛ t. pepper
1 c. chopped celery	

Melt butter in heavy skillet. Add mushrooms and cook over low heat for 5 minutes. Remove mushrooms. Add onion, parsley, and celery to skillet. Cook until onions turn yellow. Add 1/3 cup water along with wild rice and seasonings. Mix well. Add remaining water and the cooked mushrooms. Mix well. Simmer for 15 minutes. Makes 8 servings.

Darlene Kronschnabel

SWEET POTATO BAKE

5 c. mashed sweet potatoes or yams
½ t. salt
2 T. butter or margarine
1 9-oz. can pineapple tidbits (plus juice)
160 miniature marshmallows
⅓ c. pecan halves

Cut pineapple tidbits in half. Combine potatoes, salt, butter, pineapple and juice. Place half of mixture in a buttered casserole dish. Top with half of the marshmallows. Add remaining half of potato mixture. Arrange pecans on top. Cover and bake in a 350° oven for about 30 minutes. Remove cover about 10 minutes before serving. Add remaining marshmallows. Makes 6 large servings.

Hazel Hays

and there were games of skill and chance. For three days the Pilgrims and their guests gorged themselves on venison, roast duck, roast goose, clams and other shellfish, succulent eels, white bread, corn bread, leeks and watercress, and other "sallet herbes," with wild plums and dried berries as dessert—all washed down with wine, made of the wild grape both white and red, which the Pilgrims praised as "very sweet and strong." At this first Thanksgiving feast in New England, the company may have enjoyed, though there is no mention of it in the records, some of the long-legged "turkies" whose speed of foot in the woods constantly amazed the Pilgrims.

The celebration was a great success, warmly satisfying to body and soul alike, and the Pilgrims held another the next year, repeating it more or less regularly for generations.

George F. Willison

Thanksgiving Prayer

Lord, we thank Thee . . .
For precious heritage forefathers gave,
For noble ones so fearless, true and brave,
Who came to clear a wilderness unknown,
Transforming waste to a foundation stone . . .
Surviving dangers, loneliness and fears,
Looking and trusting to the future years.
This day we lift our hearts, for we are free
To sing our songs of thanks, all thanks to Thee.
We thank Thee, Lord, this heritage we know
Has come to us through Thee, and so
In humbleness we lift our hearts in prayer,
Asking Thy protection and Thy daily care.
We thank Thee, Lord . . .
For food, shelter, hearth, home, and love,
For herds, new grain, and blessings from above.
As year by year we meet in festive scenes,
Help us to know just what Thanksgiving means,
And on this day of days in bright November
Help us live true, and heritage remember,
And strive each year for better, nobler living,
Giving thanks to God, on this Thanksgiving.

Mamie Ozburn Odum

> *Our appetites have commonly confined our views of ripeness and its phenomena, color, mellowness, and perfectness, to the fruits which we eat, and we are wont to forget that an immense harvest which we do not eat, hardly use at all, is annually ripened by Nature. . . .*
>
> Henry David Thoreau

The most magnificent display of color in all the kingdom of plants is the autumnal foliage of the trees of North America. Over them all, over the clear light of the aspens and mountain ash, over the leaping flames of sumac and the hellfire flickerings of poison ivy, over the war paint of the many oaks, rise the colors of one tree—the sugar maple—in the shout of a great army. Clearest yellow, richest crimson, tumultuous scarlet, or brilliant orange—the yellow pigments shining through the over-painting of the red—the foliage of sugar maple at once outdoes and unifies the rest. It is like the mighty, marching melody that rides upon the crest of some symphonic weltering sea and, with its crying song, gives meaning to all the calculated dissonance of the orchestra.

There is no properly planted New England village without its sugar maples. They march up the hill to the old white meetinghouse and down from the high school, where the youngsters troop home laughing in the golden dusk. The falling glory light upon the shoulders of the postman, swirls after the children on roller skates, drifts through the windows of a passing bus to drop like largesse in the laps of the passengers. On a street where great maples arch, letting down their shining benediction, people seem to walk as if they had already gone to glory.

Outside the town, where the cold pure ponds gaze skyward and the white crooked brooks run whispering their sesquipedalian Indian names, the maple leaves slant drifting down to the water; there they will sink like galleons with painted sails, or spin away and away on voyages of chance that end on some little reef of feldspar and hornblende and winking mica schist. Up in the hills the hunter and his russet setter stride unharmed through these falling tongues of maple fire, that flicker in the tingling air and leap against the elemental blue of the sky where the wind is tearing crow calls to tatters.

Donald Culross Peattie

All across the country behind us—the realm of the roundheaded hardwoods, the oaks and beeches and maples—autumn's annual chromatic show was rising to its peak. Nowhere in the world are the hues more rich and varied than in the climax woodlands of the eastern United States. We could visualize the colors now, or soon to be, on plant and bush and tree all along the path we had followed: The purplish red of the Cape Cod cranberry bogs, the scarlet sheets and clouds of New England's sugar maples, the wine hue of the Cape May tupelos, the tapestry of many colors clothing the Kittitinny Ridge, the old gold of sycamores along Ohio streams, the waves of crimson running down the swamp maples beside the warbler river, the golden mittens of the sassafras in the dune country of northern Indiana. Everywhere the leaves of the third season of the year were bringing the growth of spring and summer to a dramatic rainbow end. These were the days when the flames of autumn burned most brightly in a fleeting but memorable show.

Edwin Way Teale

The base of the leaf was yellowish green, but along the sides and tip it was tinted with peach and rose—and this only the end of August! I looked at that first color as though I had never seen such beauty before that moment. It was hard to realize that the warmth now showing through had been there all the time, hidden by green chlorophyll until fading sunshine and growing cold had stopped its production. In that fallen leaf was the story of the season's advance, an indicator of shortening days and lengthening nights.

Summer comes slowly in the north, is never fully here until the end of June, and sometimes, when June is rainy and cold, it actually seems to start in July. But to have the change begin before summer has really settled down and the leaves grown to maturity is a shock when you have waited for it and dreamed about it since the snows disappeared and rivers ran free of ice.

Sigurd F. Olson

I think that the change to some higher color in a leaf is an evidence that it has arrived at a late and perfect maturity, answering to the maturity of fruits. It is generally the lowest and oldest leaves which change first. But as the perfect-winged and usually bright-colored insect is short-lived, so the leaves ripen but to fall.

Generally, every fruit, on ripening, and just before it falls, when it commences a more independent and individual existence, re-quiring less nourishment from any source, and that not so much from the earth through its stem as from the sun and air, acquires a bright tint. So do leaves. The physiologist says it is "due to an increased absorption of oxygen." That is the scientific account of the matter—only a reassertion of the fact. But I am more interested in the rosy cheek than I am to know what particular diet the maiden fed on. The very forest and herbage, the pellicle of the earth, must acquire a bright color, an evidence of its ripeness—as if the globe itself were a fruit on its stem, with ever a cheek toward the sun.

Henry David Thoreau

About the second of October, these trees, both large and small, are most brilliant, though many are still green. In "sprout-lands" they seem to vie with one another, and ever

50

some particular one in the midst of the crowd will be of a peculiarly pure scarlet, and by its more intense color attract our eye even at a distance, and carry off the palm. A large red maple swamp, when at the height of its change, is the most obviously brilliant of all tangible things, where I dwell, so abundant is this tree with us. It varies much both in form and color. A great many are merely yellow; more, scarlet; others, scarlet deepening into crimson, more red than common. Look at yonder swamp of maples mixed with pines, at the base of a pine-clad hill, a quarter of a mile off, so that you get the full effect of the bright colors, without detecting the imperfections of the leaves, and see their yellow, scarlet, and crimson fires, of all tints, mingled and contrasted with the green. Some maples are yet green, only yellow or crimson-tipped on the edges of their flakes, like the edges of a hazelnut bur; some are wholly brilliant scarlet, raying out regularly and finely every way, bilaterally, like the veins of a leaf; others, of more irregular form, when I turn my head slightly, emptying out some of its earthiness and concealing the trunk of the tree, seem to rest heavily flake on flake, like yellow and scarlet clouds, wreath upon wreath, or like snowdrifts driving through the air, stratified by the wind. It adds greatly to the beauty of such a swamp at this season, that, even though there may be no other trees interspersed, it is not seen as a simple mass of color, but, different trees being of different colors and hues, the outline of each crescent treetop is distinct, and where one laps on to another. Yet a painter would hardly venture to make them thus distinct a quarter of a mile off.

Henry David Thoreau

The hillside forest is all aglow along its edge, and in all its cracks and fissures, and soon the flames will leap upwards to the tops of the tallest trees.

Henry David Thoreau

Autumn Fires

In the other gardens
And all up the vale,
From the autumn bonfires
See the smoke trail!

Pleasant summer over,
And all the summer flowers,
The red fire blazes,
The grey smoke towers.

Sing a song of seasons!
Something bright in all!
Flowers in the summer,
Fires in the fall!

Robert Louis Stevenson

Now is the time of the illuminated woods, they have a sense of sunshine, even on a cloudy day, given by the yellow foliage; every leaf glows like a tiny lamp; one walks through their lighted halls with curious enjoyment.

John Burroughs

To the red man all these tintings of fall were of miraculous origin. They came, grew in brilliance, tarnished and faded away. It has taken the researches of a host of modern scientists to decipher the story of the painted leaves. And even so this narrative of autumn change contains a number of pages that still are blurred or partly blank.

Edwin Way Teale

The simplest of the autumn colors to explain is yellow, the gold of the aspen and the hickory and the birch. Carotene, the pigment found so abundantly in carrots, and xanthophyll, the coloring matter found in egg yolks and the feathers of the canary, are present in these leaves all summer long. In fact there is a greater quantity of these two pigments in the green leaves of midsummer than in the yellow leaves of fall. But then they are masked by the outer layers of chlorophyll.

During the warm months the tree produces and uses chlorophyll continually, with production and use balanced. Then comes the chill of autumn. It retards the production of chlorophyll more rapidly than it does its consumption. In a bleaching process that is only partly understood, the chlorophyll breaks down into colorless compounds. The green disappears from the leaf and the yellow pigments are no longer masked. Each year we see this sudden shift of autumn on elm and birch and tulip tree, the change from the green of summer to the gold of fall. The new tints we see are not new at all. They are colors that have been there all the time.

The yellows of autumn thus are produced by subtraction, the subtraction of chlorophyll. The reds of autumn are produced by addition, the addition of something that was not present in the leaf before.

From flaming scarlet to deepest purple, the most brilliant hues of the autumn woods are the products of coloring materials known as anthocyanins. They are the "cell-sap pigments." While the green of chlorophyll and the yellows of xanthophyll and carotene are contained in the protoplasm of the cell, the anthocyanins are carried in solution in the sap. Thus all the infinitely varied shades of red, the most striking feature of autumn's greatest show, are the products of tinted sap within the leaves.

Around the world and all through the vegetable kingdom the anthocyanins are distributed. They are responsible, in stem and bud and leaf and flower, for magentas and blues as well as reds and purples. . . . If the cell sap is acid the plant tends to produce bright reds. If it is alkaline it tends to produce blues and purples.

With very few exceptions—notably the garden beet, which produces its bright-red root underground—the coloring material develops only where sunshine strikes. Thus the stem end of a red apple is usually more brightly colored than the flower end which hangs down away from the sun. In experiments, opaque letters have been attached to the side of such an apple before it ripened and letters or words in green have been produced on its red surface where the skin, shielded from the sunshine, developed no anthocyanin pigment in its cells. Scientists have even printed simple photographs on apples, in varying shades of green and red, by attaching negatives to their sides during the period when the fruit was ripening.

Occasionally as we wandered through the fall we came upon a tree that was red-tinged on the outside and yellow within. The shaded leaves had failed to produce anthocyanins in sufficient quantity to make the red pigment noticeable. . . . Again, it has been noticed that the flaming colors of the sugar maple are usually brightest at the ends of the branches, where they receive the maximum amount of sunshine.

There appears to be another reason why the red of the sugar maple is the most brilliant of all. The presence of sugar in the sap is conducive to the formation of this color. When a research worker tested bright-red leaves from a Virginia creeper, he found they contained more sugar than green leaves from the same vine collected at the same time. The leaf containing the greatest amount of sugar is believed to turn the brightest red. But all summer long there is sugar in and sunshine on the leaves of the sugar maples. Yet they remain green. Why? Another factor is missing. That is cold.

When the temperature drops to forty-five degrees F., or below, it interferes with the removal of sugars and other substances from the leaves and this favors the accumulation of the pigments in the sap of the cells. A sudden drop just after the sun has set—such as occurred that last evening at Red Wing—is especially productive of brilliant autumn leaves. So are crisp, sunny days. The high, clear skies and sparkling weather that usually mark the third

season in the New World have much to do with the many-colored splendor of the forest trees.

At one time it was believed that the frost painted the autumn leaves. Now it is known that, with or without frost, lowered temperature achieves this end. In fact a hard frost or freeze early in the fall tends to destroy the yellow pigments and prevent the formation of anthocyanins. In such seasons the trees merely turn brownish without developing the reds and yellows and the infinitely varied combinations of the two. And, as every autumn progresses, even the most colorful of the painted leaves, even those of the maples that unite the ultimate brilliance of scarlet and gold and orange, they all—clinging to the tree or on the ground where they have fallen—tarnish and fade and lose their glory.

Edwin Way Teale

Ripe, red maple leaves are part of Autumn's feast for the eye.

By the twenty-fifth of September, the red maples generally are beginning to be ripe. Some large ones have been conspicuously changing for a week, and some single trees are now very brilliant. I notice a small one, half a mile off across a meadow, against the green woodside there, a far brighter red than the blossoms of any tree in summer, and more conspicuous. I have observed this tree for several autumns invariably changing earlier than its fellows, just as one tree ripens its fruit earlier than another. It might serve to mark the season, perhaps. I should be sorry if it were cut down. I know of two or three such trees in different parts of our town, which might, perhaps, be propagated from, as early ripeners or September trees, and their seed be advertised in the market, as well as that of radishes, if we cared as much about them.

At present these burning bushes stand chiefly along the edge of the meadows, or I distinguish them afar on the hillsides here and there. Sometimes you will see many small ones in a swamp turned quite crimson when all other trees around are still perfectly green, and the former appear so much the brighter for it. They take you by surprise, as you are going by on one side, across the fields, thus early in the season, as if it were some gay encampment of the red men, or other foresters, of whose arrival you had not heard.

Some single trees, wholly bright scarlet, seen against others of their kind still freshly green, or against evergreens, are more memorable than whole groves will be by and by. How beautiful, when a whole tree is like one great scarlet fruit full of ripe juices, every leaf, from lowest limb to topmost spire, all aglow, especially if you look toward the sun! What more remarkable object can there be in the landscape? Visible for miles, too fair to be believed. If such a phenomenon occurred but once, it would be handed down by tradition to posterity, and get into the mythology at last.

The whole tree thus ripening in advance of its fellows attains a singular preeminence, and sometimes maintains it for a week or two. I am thrilled at the sight of it, bearing aloft its scarlet standard for the regiment of green-clad foresters around, and I go half a mile out of my way to examine it. A single tree becomes thus the crowning beauty of some meadowy vale, and the expression of the whole surrounding forest is at once more spirited for it.

Henry David Thoreau

The maples perhaps undergo the most complete transformation of all the forest trees. Their leaves fairly become luminous, as if they glowed with inward light. In October a maple tree before your window lights up your room like a great lamp. Even on cloudy days its presence helps to dispel the gloom. The elm, the oak, the beech, possess in a much less degree that quality of luminosity, though certain species of oak at times are rich in shades of red and bronze. The leaves of the trees just named for the most part turn brown before they fall. The great leaves of the sycamore assume a rich tan color like fine leather.

John Burroughs

Land of Painted Trees

I traveled a land of painted trees,
colored by autumn's hand,
On a carpet of gold, of russet and
brown which covered the forest
land.
I gathered the leaves which fell at my
feet and tossed them into the sun,
And watched them float in the gentle
breeze, seemingly full of fun.
I stopped and gazed at the blue of the
skies through pillars of golden
hue,
And noted approaching ships of the
air reflecting the gold in the blue.
It was peaceful and calm in this silent
lane where the carol of autumn
was played.
And my heart sang out with thanks
to God for this land which his
hand had made.

Everett Wentworth Hill

But think not that the splendor of the year is over; for as one leaf does not make a summer, neither does one falling leaf make an autumn. The smallest sugar maples in our streets make a great show as early as the fifth of October, more than any other trees there. As I look up the main street, they appear like painted screens standing before the houses; yet many are green. But now, or generally by the seventeenth of October, when almost all red maples and some white maples are bare, the large sugar maples also are in their glory, glowing with yellow and red, and show unexpectedly bright and delicate tints. They are remarkable for the contrast they often afford of deep blushing red on one half and green on the other. They become at length dense masses of rich yellow with a deep scarlet blush, or more than blush, on the exposed surfaces. They are the brightest trees now in the street.

The large ones on our Common are particularly beautiful. A delicate but warmer than golden yellow is now the prevailing color, with scarlet cheeks. Yet, standing on the east side of the Common just before sundown, when the western light is transmitted through them, I see that their yellow even, compared with the pale lemon yellow of an elm close by, amounts to a scarlet, without noticing the bright scarlet portions. Generally, they are great regular oval masses of yellow and scarlet. All the sunny warmth of the season, the Indian summer, seems to be absorbed in their leaves. The lowest and inmost leaves next the bole are, as usual, of the most delicate yellow and green, like the complexion of young men brought up in the house. There is an auction on the Common today, but its red flag is hard to be discerned amid this blaze of color.

Henry David Thoreau

Belonging to a genus which is remarkable for the beautiful form of its leaves, I suspect that some scarlet oak leaves surpass those of all other oaks in the rich and wild beauty of their outlines. I judge from an acquaintance with twelve species, and from drawings which I have seen of many others.

Stand under this tree and see how finely its leaves are cut against the sky—as it were, only a few sharp points extending from a midrib. They look like double, treble, or quadruple crosses. They are far more ethereal than the less deeply scalloped oak leaves. They have so little leafy *terra firma* that they appear melting away in the light, and scarcely obstruct our view. . . .

· I am again struck with their beauty, when, a month later, they thickly strew the ground in the woods, piled one upon another under my feet. They are then brown above, but purple beneath. With their narrow lobes and their bold, deep scallops reaching almost to the middle, they suggest that the material must be cheap, or else there has been a lavish expense in their creation, as if so much had been cut out. Or else they seem to us the remnants of the stuff out of which leaves have been cut with a die. Indeed, when they lie thus one upon another, they remind me of a pile of scrap-tin.

Henry David Thoreau

By the twenty-sixth of October the large scarlet oaks are in their prime, when other oaks are usually withered. They have been kindling their fires for a week past, and now generally burst into a blaze. This alone of our indigenous deciduous trees (excepting the dogwood, of which I do not know half a dozen, and they are but large bushes) is now in its glory. The two aspens and the sugar maple come nearest to it in date, but they have lost the greater part of their leaves. Of evergreens, only the pitch pine is still commonly bright.

But it requires a particular alertness, if not devotion to these phenomena, to appreciate the widespread, but late and unexpected glory of the scarlet oaks. I do not speak here of the small trees and shrubs, which are commonly observed, and which are now withered, but of the large trees. Most go in and shut their doors, thinking that bleak and colorless November has already come, when some of the most brilliant and memorable colors are not yet lit.

Henry David Thoreau

Already, by the first of September, I had seen two or three small maples turned scarlet across the pond, beneath where the white stems of three aspens diverged, at the point of a promontory, next the water. Ah, many a tale their color told! And gradually from week to week the character of each tree came out, and it admired itself reflected in the

These bright leaves which I have mentioned are not the exception, but the rule; for I believe that all leaves, even grasses and mosses, acquire brighter colors just before their fall. When you come to observe faithfully the changes of each humblest plant, you find that each has, sooner or later, its peculiar autumnal tint; and if you undertake to make a complete list of the bright tints, it will be nearly as long as a catalogue of the plants in your vicinity.

Henry David Thoreau

smooth mirror of the lake. Each morning the manager of this gallery substituted some new picture, distinguished by more brilliant or harmonious coloring, for the old upon the walls.

The intense brilliancy of the red-ripe maples scattered here and there in the midst of the green oaks and hickories on the hilly shore of Walden is quite charming. They are unexpectedly and incredibly brilliant, especially on the western shore and close to the water's edge, where, alternating with yellow branches and poplars and green oaks, they remind me of a line of soldiers, redcoats and riflemen in green mixed together.

Henry David Thoreau

Looking across this woodland valley, a quarter of a mile wide, how rich those scarlet oaks embosomed in pines, their bright red branches intimately intermingled with them! They have their full effect there. The pine boughs are the green calyx to their red petals. Or, as we go along a road in the woods, the sun striking endwise through it, and lighting up the red tents of the oaks, which on each side are mingled with the liquid green of the pines, makes a very gorgeous scene. Indeed, without the evergreens for contrast, the autumnal tints would lose much of their effect.

Henry David Thoreau

> *" . . . the pine sheds
> its leaves period-
> ically, though always
> as it were stealthily
> and under cover of
> new foliage."*
>
> John Burroughs

Nature has many scenes to exhibit, and constantly draws a curtain over this part or that. She is constantly repainting the landscape and all surfaces, dressing up some scene for our entertainment. Lately we had a leafy wilderness; now bare twigs begin to prevail, and soon she will surprise us with a mantle of snow. Some green she thinks so good for our eyes that, like blue, she never banishes it entirely from our eyes, but has created evergreens.

Henry David Thoreau

The evergreens can keep a secret the year round, someone has said. How well they keep the secret of the shedding of their leaves! so well that in the case of the spruces we hardly know when it does occur. In fact, the spruces do not properly shed their leaves at all, but simply outgrow them, after carrying them an indefinite time. Some of the species carry their leaves five or six years. The hemlock drops its leaves very irregularly: the winds and the storms whip them off; in winter the snow beneath them is often covered with them.

But the pine sheds its leaves periodically, though always as it were stealthily and under cover of the newer foliage. The white pine usually sheds its leaves in midsummer, though I have known all the pines to delay till October. It is on with the new love before it is off with the old. From May till near autumn it carries two crops of leaves, last year's and the present year's. Emerson's inquiry,

How the sacred pine-tree adds
To her old leaves new myriads,

is framed in strict accordance with the facts. It is to her *old* leaves that she adds the new. Only the new growth, the outermost leaves, are

carried over till the next season, thus keeping the tree always clothed and green. As its moulting season approaches, these old leaves, all the rear ranks on the limbs, begin to turn yellow, and a careless observer might think the tree was struck with death, but it is not. The decay stops just where the growth of the previous spring began, and presently the tree stands green and vigorous, with a newly-laid carpet of fallen leaves beneath it.

John Burroughs

A great part of the pine needles have just fallen. See the carpet of pale-brown needles under this pine. How light it lies upon the grass, and that great rock, and the wall, resting thick on its top and its shelves, and on the bushes and underwood, hanging lightly! They are not yet flat and reddish, but a more delicate pale brown, and lie up light as joggle-sticks, just dropped. The ground is nearly concealed by them. How beautifully they die, making cheerfully their annual contribution to the soil! They fall to rise again; as if they knew that it was not one annual deposit alone that made this rich mold in which pine trees grow.

They live in the soil whose fertility and bulk they increase, and in the forests that spring from it.

Henry David Thoreau

Both the pine and the hemlock make friends with the birch, the maple, and the oak, and one of the most pleasing and striking features of our autumnal scenery is a mountain side sown broadcast with these intermingled trees, forming a combination of colors like the richest tapestry, the dark green giving body and permanence, the orange and yellow giving light and brilliancy.

John Burroughs

It is indeed a golden autumn. These ten days are enough to make the reputation of any climate. A tradition of these days might be handed down to posterity. They deserve a notice in history, in the history of Concord. All kinds of crudities have a chance to get ripe this year. Was there ever such an autumn? . . .

Sat in the old pasture beyond the Corner Spring woods to look at that pine wood now at the height of its change, pitch and white. Their change produces a very singular and pleasing effect. They are regularly parti-colored. The last year's leaves about a foot beneath the extremities of the twigs on all sides, now changed and ready to fall, have their period of brightness as well as broader leaves. They are a clear yellow, contrasting with the fresh and liquid green of the terminal plumes, or this year's leaves. These quite distinct colors are regularly and equally distributed over the whole tree. You have the warmth of the yellow and the coolness of the green. So it should be with our own maturity, not yellow to the very extremity of our shoots, but youthful and untried green ever putting forth afresh at the extremities, foretelling a maturity as yet unknown. The ripe leaves fall to the ground, and become nutriment for the green ones which still aspire to heaven. In the fall of the leaf there is no fruit, there is no true maturity, neither in our science and wisdom.

Henry David Thoreau

The leaves are gone from the hillsides and the glory of the red maple and of the yellow aspen and birch is strewn upon the ground. Only in the protected swamps is there any color, the smoky gold of the tamaracks. A week ago those trees were yellow, but now they are dusty and tarnished.

Sigurd F. Olson

In that little leaf was all the poetry of fall, the first soft prelude of the symphony just finished. The cycle was complete once more. Now the snows could come.

The time of the falling of leaves has come again. Once more in our morning walk we tread upon carpets of gold and crimson, of brown and bronze, woven by the winds or the rains out of these delicate textures while we slept.

How beautifully the leaves grow old! How full of light and color are their last days! There are exceptions, of course. The leaves of most of the fruit trees fade and wither and fall ingloriously. They bequeath their heritage of color to their fruit. Upon it they lavish the hues which other trees lavish upon their leaves. The pear tree is often an exception. I have seen pear orchards in October painting a hillside in hues of mingled bronze and gold. And well may the pear tree do this, it is so chary of color upon its fruit.

But in October what a feast to the eye our woods and groves present! The whole body of the air seems enriched by their calm, slow radiance. They are giving back the light they have been absorbing from the sun all summer.

The carpet of the newly fallen leaves looks so clean and delicate when it first covers the paths and the highways that one almost hesitates to walk upon it. Was it the gallant Raleigh who threw down his cloak for Queen Elizabeth to walk upon? See what a robe the maples have thrown down for you and me to walk upon! How one hesitates to soil it!

John Burroughs

By the sixth of October the leaves generally begin to fall, in successive showers, after frost or rain; but the principal leaf-harvest, the acme of the Fall, is commonly about the sixteenth. Some morning at that date there is perhaps a harder frost than we have seen, and ice formed under the pump, and now, when the morning wind rises, the leaves come down in denser showers than ever. They suddenly form thick beds or carpets on the ground, in this gentle air, or even without wind, just the size and form of the tree above. Some trees, as small hickories, appear to have dropped their leaves instantaneously, as a soldier grounds arms at a signal; and those of the hickory, being bright yellow still, though withered, reflect a blaze of light from the ground where they lie. Down they have come on all sides, at the first earnest touch of autumn's wand, making a sound like rain.

Or else it is after moist and rainy weather that we notice how great a fall of leaves there has been in the night, though it may not yet be the touch that loosens the rock maple leaf. The streets are thickly strewn with the trophies, and fallen elm leaves make a dark brown pavement under our feet. After some remarkably warm Indian-summer day or days, I perceive that it is the unusual heat which, more than anything, causes the leaves to fall, there having been, perhaps, no frost nor rain for some time. The intense heat suddenly ripens and wilts them, just as it softens and ripens peaches and other fruits, and causes them to drop.

The leaves of late red maples, still bright, strew the earth, often crimson-spotted on a yellow ground, like some wild apples—though they preserve these bright colors on the ground but a day or two, especially if it rains. On causeways I go by trees here and there all bare and smoke-like, having lost their brilliant clothing; but there it lies, nearly as bright as ever, on the ground on one side, and making nearly as regular a figure as lately on the tree. I would rather say that I first observe the trees thus flat on the ground like a permanent colored shadow, and they suggest to look for the boughs that bore them. A queen might be proud to walk where these gallant trees have spread their bright cloaks in the mud. I see wagons roll over them as a shadow or a reflection, and the drivers heed them just as little as they did their shadows before.

Birds' nests, in the huckleberry and other shrubs, and in trees, are already being filled with the withered leaves. So many have fallen in the woods that a squirrel cannot run after a falling nut without being heard. Boys are raking them in the streets, if only for the pleasure of dealing with such clean, crisp substances. Some sweep the paths scrupulously neat, and then stand to see the next breath strew them with new trophies.

Henry David Thoreau

How they are mixed up, of all species, oak and maple and chestnut and birch! But Nature is not cluttered with them; she is a perfect husbandman; she stores them all. Consider what a vast crop is thus annually shed on the earth! This, more than any mere grain or seed, is the great harvest of the year. The trees are now repaying the earth with interest what they have taken from it. They are discounting. They are about to add a leaf's thickness to the depth of the soil. This is the beautiful way in which Nature gets her muck, while I chaffer with this man and that, who talks to me about sulphur and the cost of carting. We are all the

richer for their decay. I am more interested in this crop than in the English grass alone or in the corn. It prepares the virgin mould for future cornfields and forests, on which the earth fattens. It keeps our homestead in good heart.

For beautiful variety no crop can be compared with this. Here is not merely the plain yellow of the grains, but nearly all the colors that we know, the brightest blue not excepted: the early blushing maple, the poison sumach blazing its sins as scarlet, the mulberry ash, the rich chrome yellow of the poplars, the brilliant red huckleberry, with which the hills' backs are painted, like those of sheep. The frost touches them, and, with the slightest breath of returning day or jarring of earth's axle, see in what showers they come floating down! The ground is all parti-colored with them. But they

The ponds and streams bear upon their bosoms leaves of all tints, from the deep maroon of the oak to the pale yellow of the chestnut.

John Burroughs

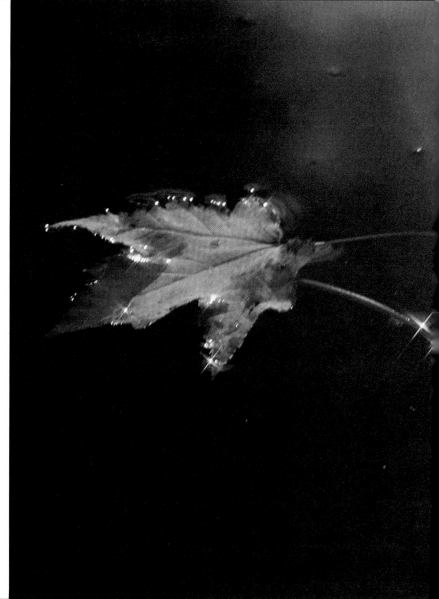

still live in the soil, whose fertility and bulk they increase, and in the forests that spring from it. They stoop to rise, to mount higher in coming years, by subtle chemistry, climbing by the sap in the trees; and the sapling's first fruits thus shed, transmuted at last, may adorn its crown, when, in after years, it has become the monarch of the forest.

It is pleasant to walk over the beds of these fresh, crisp, and rustling leaves. How beautifully they go to their graves! how gently lay themselves down and turn to mould!—painted of a thousand hues, and fit to make the beds of us living. So they troop to their last resting-place, light and frisky. They put on no weeds, but merrily they go scampering over the earth, selecting the spot, choosing a lot, ordering no iron fence, whispering all through the woods about it—some choosing the spot where the

bodies of men are mouldering beneath, and meeting them halfway. How many flutterings before they rest quietly in their graves! They that soared so loftily, how contentedly they return to dust again, and are laid low, resigned to lie and decay at the foot of the tree, and afford nourishment to new generations of their kind, as well as to flutter on high! They teach us how to die. One wonders if the time will ever come when men, with their boasted faith in immortality, will lie down as gracefully and as ripe—with such an Indian-summer serenity will shed their bodies, as they do their hair and nails.

Henry David Thoreau

Perchance, in the afternoon of such a day, when the water is perfectly calm and full of reflections, I paddle gently down the main stream, and turning up the Assabet, reach a quiet cove, where I unexpectedly find myself surrounded by myriads of leaves, like fellow-voyagers, which seem to have the same purpose, or want of purpose, with myself. See this great fleet of scattered leaf-boats which we paddle amid, in this smooth river-bay, each one curled up on every side by the sun's skill, each nerve a stiff spruce knee—like boats of hide, and of all patterns—Charon's boat probably among the rest—and some with lofty prows and poops, like the stately vessels of the ancients, scarcely moving in the sluggish current—like the great fleets, the dense Chinese cities of boats, with which you mingle on entering some great mart, some New York or Canton, which we are all steadily approaching together. How gently each has been deposited on the water! No violence has been used towards them yet, though, perchance, palpitating hearts were present at the launching. And painted ducks, too, the splendid wood duck among the rest, often come to sail and float amid the painted leaves—barks of a nobler model still!

Henry David Thoreau

There are many crisped but colored leaves resting on the smooth surface of the Assabet, which for the most part is not stirred by a breath; but in some places, where the middle is rippled by a slight breeze, no leaves are seen, while the broad and perfectly smooth

How much beauty in decay! I pick up a white oak leaf, dry and stiff, but yet mingled red and green, October-like, whose pulpy part some insect has eaten beneath, exposing the delicate network of its veins. It is very beautiful held up to the light—such work as only an insect eye could perform. Yet, perchance, to the vegetable kingdom such a revelation of ribs is as repulsive as the skeleton in the animal kingdom. In each case it is some little gourmand, working for another end, that reveals the wonders of nature. There are countless oak leaves in this condition now, and also with a submarginal line of network exposed.

Henry David Thoreau

portions next the shore will be covered with them, as if by a current they were prevented from falling on the other parts. These leaves are chiefly of the red maple, with some white maple, etc. To be sure, they hardly begin to conceal the river, unless in some quiet coves, yet they remind me of ditches in swamps, whose surfaces are often quite concealed by leaves now. The waves made by my boat cause them to rustle, and both by sounds and sights I am reminded that I am in the very midst of the fall.

Methinks the reflections are never purer and more distinct than now at the season of the fall of the leaf, just before the cool twilight has come, when the air has a finer grain. Just as our mental reflections are more distinct at this season of the year, when the evenings grow cool and lengthen and our winter evenings with their brighter fires may be said to begin.

Henry David Thoreau

But along the roadsides and underneath the trees now appeared a display that until then had been hidden from view. Cherries, mountain maple, Juneberry, honeysuckle, and hazel all had turned to shades of red and gold. Blueberry and bearberry beneath the pines were now a carpet of crimson. Together with the fallen leaves, they made the entire forest floor a tapestry of color even richer and more varied than the trees had been. Now for the first time one could look through the woods and far into them with vistas that seemed to stretch on endlessly into more and more color.

Even the bogs began to turn from their summer's green and brown to tones of copper, each muskeg a soft carpet, the heathers blending together to complement the brilliant shrubs that hemmed them close.

The rice beds in rivers and swampy bays were yellow against the blue. Portages were deep in leaves, for all the glory that had been was on the ground. For a month the color had been almost more than could be borne. Senses had been surfeited by overwhelming beauty. Now at last the somberness could come and eyes could rest and minds as well.

Sigurd F. Olson

. . . the sound grew louder, changed in a moment from a vague, blended harmony to the clear, joyous clamor of birds coming in to feed.

Sigurd F. Olson

It was November and I was on top of a high, birch-covered ridge. The air was rich with the smell of down leaves and the ground was covered with bronze and tarnished gold. Far below was a blue lake with a rice-filled river flowing into it. Where the river met the open water, the rice fanned out like a golden apron, solidly colored at the gathered waist, flecked with blue toward its fringes.

Suddenly out of the north came the sound I had been waiting for, a soft, melodious gabbling that swelled and died and increased in volume until all other sounds were engulfed by its clamor. Far in the blue I saw them, a long skein of dots undulating like a floating ribbon pulled toward the south by an invisible cord tied to the point of its V.

Sigurd F. Olson

Another time, when the sun was setting over the marshes of Totagatik Lake, the wild gabbling came out of the north and the birds were silhouetted against a flaming sky. That time they caught me in the open between the rice and the tall grass near shore, but it was dusk and the canoe blended into its background. That instant is burned into my memory: the water like wine, the approaching flock, black spruce etched against the sky. Then they came, down—down—down out of the gloom until I could feel the measured beat of their wings.

Sigurd F. Olson

That day started with the uncertain crows. It ended with the cautious Canada geese. Between the two it was filled with a long succession of flocks and waves and concentrations of many kinds of birds. The full tide of migration now was flowing down the valley of the Missouri to join the mightier tide of the Mississippi Flyway. For more than 150 miles that day, we overtook and moved among wave after wave of migrants. It was as though we

High overhead the wild geese soar,
And, oh, that I with them could fly
Far from the crowded haunts of man
Against a cloudless autumn sky!

Their shadow on the pallid moon
That dims the cold stars from my sight
Are wings on which my heart would fly
Away into an unknown night.

Wild geese, wild geese, where do you go?
Is yours always an endless quest
Through boundless solitude on high?
Is yours the heart that knows no rest?

Your trumpet call comes to my ears
At night within my lonely bed.
But I must stay when heart would go;
I cannot heed your call o'erhead.

High in the sky the wild geese soar,
And, oh, that I with them could fly
Far from the crowded haunts of man,
Against a cloudless autumn sky!

William Arnette Wofford

Through the sun-shine and drifting milkweed fluff and gossamer showers of this autumn day we saw a million ducks.

Edwin Way Teale

Not only are birds at their peak in numbers in the fall but they are at their peak in weight. If you could weigh the southbound migrants of an American autumn, you would have more pounds of birds than at any other time of year.

Edwin Way Teale

were riding a surfboard, sweeping ahead on the crests of the great combers of the autumn flight.

Edwin Way Teale

One after the other, half a dozen times in the course of the day, we overtook long, straggling, southward-drifting flocks of crows. One, like a skein of windblown smoke, was strung out for more than a mile. A whole flock had landed across one hillside, and at another place the black birds of passage were crowding around a water hole to drink. Big hawks, too, were on the move. Most seemed to be rough-legs and that hawk of the prairies, Swainson's, but a number were redtails. Usually we saw them soaring southward or circling in the sky

but there was one yellow slope, descending to a swale bordered by green-black rushes, where almost every one of the gray, scattered rocks held a perching Buteo.

Edwin Way Teale

It was late October and the tamaracks were as golden as they would ever be. Before me was a stand of wild rice, yellow against the water, and because it was a bluebird day there was not a wing in the sky. I stood there just looking at the horizon. Suddenly the sun went under a cloud and it began to snow, softly at first, and then as the wind rose the serrated ranks of tamaracks across the bay almost disappeared in swirling flakes. A flock of northern bluebills tore out of the sky with that canvas-

ponds and the river, like black motes in the sky; and, when I thought they had gone off thither long since, they would settle down by a slanting flight of a quarter of a mile onto a distant part which was left free; but what beside safety they got by sailing in the middle of Walden I do not know, unless they love its water for the same reason that I do.

Henry David Thoreau

But summer wanes, and autumn approaches. The songsters of the seedtime are silent at the reaping of the harvest. Other minstrels take up the strain. It is the heyday of insect life. The day is canopied with musical sound. All the songs of the spring and summer appear to be floating, softened and refined, in the upper air. The birds, in a new but less holiday suit, turn their faces southward. The swallows flock and go; the bobolinks flock and go; silently and unobserved, the thrushes go. Autumn arrives, bringing finches, warblers, sparrows, and kinglets from the north. Silently the procession passes. Yonder hawk, sailing peacefully away till he is lost in the horizon, is a symbol of the closing season and the departing birds.

John Burroughs

ripping sound that only bluebills make when they have been riding the tail of the wind and decide to come in. In a split second, an instant in which I was too startled even to move, there were a hundred wings where before there had been nothing but space. Then they were gone and in the same instant the sun came out.

Sigurd F. Olson

For hours, in fall days, I watched the ducks cunningly tack and veer and hold the middle of the pond, far from the sportsmen; tricks which they will have less need to practice in Louisiana bayous. When compelled to rise they would sometimes circle round and round and over the pond at a considerable height, from which they could easily see to other

The nighthawk circled overhead in the sunny afternoon—for I sometimes made a day of it—like a mote in the eye, or in heaven's eye, falling from time to time with a swoop and a sound as if the heavens were rent, torn at last to very rags and tatters, and yet a seamless cope remained; small imps that fill the air and lay their eggs on the ground on bare sand or rocks on the tops of hills, where few have found them; graceful and slender like ripples caught up from the pond, as leaves are raised by the wind to float in the heavens; such kindredship is in nature. The hawk is aerial brother of the wave which he sails over and surveys, those his perfect air-inflated wings answering to the elemental unfledged pinions of the sea. Or sometimes I watched a pair of hen hawks circling high in the sky, alternately soaring and descending, approaching and leaving one another, as if they were the embodiment of my own thoughts.

Henry David Thoreau

Chinese Chestnuts.

When chestnuts were ripe I laid up half a bushel for winter. It was very exciting at that season to roam the then boundless chestnut woods of Lincoln—they now sleep their long sleep under the railroad—with a bag on my shoulder, and stick to open burs with in my hand, for I did not always wait for the frost, amid the rustling of leaves and the loud reproofs of the red squirrels and the jays, whose half-consumed nuts I sometimes stole, for the burs which they had selected were sure to contain sound ones. Occasionally I climbed and shook the trees. They grew also behind my house, and one large tree, which almost overshadowed it, was, when in flower, a bouquet which scented the whole neighborhood, but the squirrels and the jays got most of its fruit; the last coming in flocks early in the morning and picking the nuts out of the burs before they fell. I relinquished these trees to them and visited the more distant woods composed wholly of chestnut. These nuts, as far as they went, were a good substitute for bread.

Henry David Thoreau

I can see the woods in their autumn dress, the oaks purple, the hickories washed with gold, the maples and sumachs luminous with crimson fires, and I can hear the rustle made by the fallen leaves as we plowed through them. I can see the blue clusters of wild grapes hanging among the foliage of the saplings, and I remember the taste of them and the smell. I know how the wild blackberries looked, and how they tasted, and the same with the pawpaws, the hazelnuts, and the persimmons; and I can feel the thumping rain, upon my head, of hickory nuts and walnuts when we were out in the frosty dawn to scramble for them with the pigs, and the gusts of wind loosed them and sent them down.

I know the delicate art and mystery of so cracking hickory nuts and walnuts on a flatiron with a hammer that the kernels will be delivered whole, and I know how the nuts, taken in conjunction with winter apples, cider and doughnuts, make old people's old tales and old jokes sound fresh and crisp and enchanting, and juggle an evening away before you know what went with the time.

Mark Twain

70

On some still day in autumn, one of the nutty days, the woods will often be pervaded by an undertone of sound, produced by their multitudinous clucking, as they sit near their dens. It is one of the characteristic sounds of fall.

I was much amused one October in watching a chipmunk carry nuts and other food into his den. He had made a well-defined path from his door out through the weeds and dry leaves into the territory where his feeding ground lay. The path was a crooked one; it dipped under weeds, under some large, loosely piled stones, under a pile of chestnut posts, and then followed the remains of an old wall. Going and coming, his motions were like clockwork. He always went by spurts and sudden sallies. He was never for one moment off his guard. He would appear at the mouth of his den, look quickly about, take a few leaps to a tussock of grass, pause a breath with one foot raised, slip quickly a few yards over some dry leaves, pause again by a stump beside a path, rush across the path to the pile of loose stones, go under the first and over the second, gain the pile of posts, make his way through that, survey his course a half moment from the other side of it, and then dart on to some other cover, and presently beyond my range, where I think he gathered acorns, as there were no other nut-bearing trees than oaks near.

John Burroughs

Gathering Nuts in Fall

When summer is over and turned into fall;
When wild geese are honking; when bluejays call;
When mornings are crisp it is time then, I know;
The nut trees are loaded and it's time to go.

Then I love to remember the old-fashioned scene,
When we'd get bags and baskets and hitch up the team
And head for the woods, where we always knew
The walnuts, the beechnuts, and hickory nuts grew.

For beechnuts we'd spread old sheets on the ground,
Then shake the limbs where the best nuts were found,
Then laugh with glee as the nuts start to shower,
Getting more in a minute than you could pick in an hour.

Getting walnuts and hickories was harder to do;
But with old clubs, which we accurately threw,
They rained down in plenty with a plupity-plup,
And waiting hands greedily gathered them up.

I love to recall those dear days of old,
When we gathered nuts we thought good as gold;
For they added a treat to a long, winter night,
As we ate nuts and apples where hearth fires burned bright.

Ernest Jack Sharpe

Walnuts.

Hazelnuts.

Butternut.

Shagbark Hickory nuts.

The cheeks of the red and gray squirrels are made without pockets, and whatever they transport is carried in the teeth. They are more or less active all winter, but October and November are their festal months. Invade some butternut or hickory grove on a frosty October morning, and hear the red squirrel beat the "juba" on a horizontal branch. It is a most lively jig, what the boys call a "regular break-down," interspersed with squeals and snickers and derisive laughter.

John Burroughs

His career of frolic and festivity begins in the fall, after the birds have left us and the holiday spirit of nature has commenced to subside. How much his presence adds to the pleasure of a saunter in the still October woods. You step lightly across the threshold of the forest, and sit down upon the first log or rock to await the signals. It is so still that the ear suddenly seems to have acquired new powers, and there is no movement to confuse the eye. Presently you hear the rustling of a branch, and see it sway or spring as the squirrel leaps from or to it; or else you hear a disturbance in the dry leaves, and mark one running upon the

"The squirrels career of frolic and festivity begins in the fall."

John Burroughs

. . . he mounts a stump to see if the way is clear, then pauses a moment at the foot of a tree to take his bearings, tail as he skims along undulating behind him, and adding to the easy grace and dignity of his movements.

John Burroughs

ground. He has probably seen the intruder, and, not liking his stealthy movements, desires to avoid a nearer acquaintance. Now he mounts a stump to see if the way is clear, then pauses a moment at the foot of a tree to take his bearings, his tail as he skims along undulating behind him, and adding to the easy grace and dignity of his movements. Or else you are first advised of his proximity by the dropping of a false nut, or the fragments of the shucks rattling upon the leaves. Or, again, after contemplating you a while unobserved, and making up his mind that you are not dangerous, he strikes an attitude on a branch, and commences to quack

and bark, with an accompanying movement of his tail.

John Burroughs

There is one thing the red squirrel knows unerringly that I do not (there are probably several other things); that is, on which side of the butternut the meat lies. He always gnaws through the shell so as to strike the kernel broadside, and thus easily extract it; while to my eyes there is no external mark or indication, in the form or appearance of the nut, as there is in the hickorynut, by which I can tell whether the edge or the side of the meat is toward me. But examine any number of nuts that the squirrels have rifled, and, as a rule, you will find they always drill through the shell at the one spot where the meat will be most exposed. Occasionally one makes a mistake, but not often. It stands them in hand to know, and they do know. Doubtless, if butternuts were a main source of my food, and I were compelled to gnaw into them, I should learn, too, on which side my bread was buttered.

John Burroughs

The woodchuck usually burrows on a sidehill. This enables him to guard against being drowned out, by making the termination of the hole higher than the entrance. He digs in slantingly for about two or three feet, then makes a sharp upward turn and keeps nearly parallel with the surface of the ground for a distance of eight or ten feet farther, according to the grade. Here he makes his nest and passes the winter, holing up in October or November and coming out again in March or April. This is a long sleep, and is rendered possible only by the amount of fat with which the system has become stored during the summer. The fire of life still burns, but very faintly and slowly, as with the draughts all closed and the ashes heaped up. Respiration is continued, but at longer intervals, and all the vital processes are nearly at a standstill. Dig one out during hibernation (Audubon did so), and you find it a mere inanimate ball, that suffers itself to be moved and rolled about without showing signs of awakening. But bring it in by the fire, and it presently unrolls and opens its eyes, and crawls feebly about, and if left to itself will seek some dark hole or corner, roll itself up again, and resume its former condition.

John Burroughs

A black bear begins hibernation in its den.

By mid-October most of the Rip Van Winkles among our brute creatures have lain down for their winter nap. The toads and turtles have buried themselves in the earth. The woodchuck is in his hibernaculum, the skunk in his, the mole in his; and the black bear has his selected and will go in when the snow comes. He does not like the looks of his big tracks in the snow. They publish his goings and comings too plainly. The coon retires about the same time. The provident wood mice and the chipmunk are laying by a winter supply of nuts or grain, the former usually in decayed trees, the latter in the ground.

John Burroughs

Although scientists have been studying the mystery sleep of the hibernating animal for hundreds of years it is still largely a puzzle unsolved. Like the riddle of migration among birds, its effect is obvious; but its hidden causes and its exact manner of functioning are relatively unknown. Both migration and hibernation enable creatures to live winterless lives, to escape the effects of cold and scarcity of food. Both are nature's schemes for keeping alive, in a given area, more creatures than there is food to feed the year round.

What induces hibernation? What trigger sets it off? It is not always cold although cold is usually a factor. Most of the long sleepers have disappeared by the time the mercury falls to fifty degrees F. But woodchucks frequently den up while it is still comparatively warm and some ground squirrels commence their hibernation as early as midsummer—beginning a sleep that may last for thirty-three of the fifty-two weeks of the year. Moreover daily readings of a thermometer placed in a woodchuck burrow revealed that the lowest temperatures came late in winter at a time when the animal was waking up.

Nor is the main cause scarcity of food. Animals in captivity often drowse off into their winter slumber with ample food beside them. Nor is the single explanation the lessening light of the shortening days. For hibernators nod and fall asleep in well-lighted, well-ventilated laboratories. Under wild conditions cold, hunger, darkness, quiet all seem important to hibernation. But there is no one cause known. Moreover, just as only certain birds have the instinctive urge to migrate, so only the hibernators among animals have the racial rhythm that leads to winter torpor.

Edwin Way Teale

That sleep, the deathlike torpor of hibernation, was drawing near for a host of other creatures. Already most of the Richardson's ground squirrels, those widespread rodents that are the source of North Dakota's nickname, The Flickertail State, were drowsing in their burrows. We saw only a few, at rare intervals, sitting upright like tent pegs beside the road. Somewhere west of the Red River Valley, as we had moved out across the prairie, we had passed through the vague, shadowy western borderline of the woodchuck's range. Behind it, all the way from Maine to Minnesota, these pastureland marmots were sleek and fat, curling up in their underground rooms, closing their eyes, breathing ever more slowly, their heart beats separated by greater and greater intervals. Undisturbed by wind or sleet or blizzard, unaware of cold or scarcity of food, the woodchuck and its fellow sleepers would spend the winter wrapped in the profoundest of slumbers.

This dropping into a sleep that seems so close to death is one of the strangest adventures of the animal world. The flame of life, for months on end, sinks so low it almost—but not quite—goes out.

During the summer a woodchuck breathes between twenty-five and thirty times a minute, reaching a hundred times a minute when excited. Yet, during hibernation, it may breathe only once in five minutes. Normally its heart throbs about eighty times a minute. In emergencies it may jump to two hundred times a minute. During the long sleep of hibernation, however, its pulse may slow down to four or five beats a minute, just sufficient to keep its thickened and sluggish blood in motion. Its limbs grow rigid. Even though, like all hibernating animals, it rolls itself into a ball to conserve heat, its temperature drops as low as thirty-seven degrees F., only five degrees above freezing. Thus for months on end—for as much as five months and sometimes more—the hibernating woodchuck skirts the fine line that divides the living and the dead.

Edwin Way Teale

It will be a bad winter if:
Squirrels begin gathering nuts early (middle or late September).
Muskrat houses are built big.
Beaver lodges have more logs.
The north side of a beaver dam is more covered with sticks than the south.
Squirrels' tails grow bushier.
Fur or hair on animals such as horses, sheep, mules, cows, and dogs is thicker than usual.
The fur on the bottom of rabbit's foot is thicker.
Cows' hooves break off earlier.
Squirrels build nests low in trees.
Wild hogs gather sticks, straw, and shucks to make a bed.
Animals grow a short fuzzy coat under their regular one.
Crows gather together.
Hoot owls call late in the fall.
Screech owls sound like women crying.
Juncos are feeding the trees.
Birds huddle on the ground.
You hear an "old hoot owl on the mountain, winter's comin' soon—better put on your boots"—Kenny Runion.
Birds eat up all the berries early.

Now the Deer Come Back

Now the deer come back with the season
  turning yellow,
Now the days run short and the grass
  is thin,
Now that the west holds haze and the
  sun is mellow;
Here in the field are tracks where the
  deer have been.
They must have stepped on frost this
  early morning,
Making their way to the rocky haw-lined
  creek,
Stopping to sniff the air and lightly
  scorning
Our silent smokeless house on the hill's
  tan cheek.
This is the place they crossed, and
  here they halted,
Leaving sharp marks in the mud along
  the bank,
This is the way they took, this fence
  they vaulted
And here the footprints end where the
  shrub grows rank;
And to think we slept so near, yet so
  unknowing
This beauty, and the silence of its going!

A. L. Fisher

One of the annual signs of autumn on this mountainside is the movement of the Columbian black-tailed deer down from the higher levels. In spring they climb the slopes after the retreating snow. They spend the summer among the high mountain meadows free from the multitude of flies that infest the lowland woods. Some, particularly the older bucks, range even above the timberline. Then with the first heavy snows of autumn the deer move down to the valleys again. Year after year, following the same trails each time, they engage in this definite seasonal and altitudinal migration.

Edwin Way Teale

Animal life parallels human life at many points, but it is in another plane. Something guides the lower animals, but it is not thought; something restrains them, but it is not judgment; they are provident without prudence; they are active without industry; they are skillful without practice; they are wise without knowledge; they are rational without reason; they are deceptive without guile. They cross seas without a compass, they return home without guidance, they communicate without language, their flocks act as a unit without signals or leaders. When they are joyful, they sing or they play; when they are distressed, they moan or they cry; when they are jealous, they bite or they claw, or they strike or they

gore—and yet I do not suppose they experience the emotions of joy or sorrow, or anger or love, as we do, because these feelings in them do not involve reflection, memory, and what we call the higher nature, as with us.

The animals do not have to consult the almanac to know when to migrate or to go into winter quarters. At a certain time in the fall, I see the newts all making for the marshes; at a certain time in the spring, I see them all returning to the woods again. At one place where I walk, I see them on the railroad track wandering up and down between the rails, trying to get across. I often lend them a hand. They know when and in what direction to go, but not in the way I should know under the same circumstances. I should have to learn or be told: they know instinctively.

John Burroughs

I think I could turn and live with animals,
    they are so placid and self-contain'd,
I stand and look at them long and long.

They do not sweat and whine about their condition,
They do not lie awake in the dark and weep for their sins,
They do not make me sick discussing their duty to God,
Not one is dissatisfied, not one is demented
    with the mania of owning things,
Not one kneels to another, nor to his kind
    that lived thousands of years ago,
Not one is respectable or unhappy over the whole earth.

Walt Whitman

November

Yet one smile more, departing, distant sun!
One mellow smile through the soft vapory air,
Ere, o'er the frozen earth, the loud winds run,
Or snows are sifted o'er the meadows bare.
One smile on the brown hills and naked trees,
And the dark rocks whose summer wreaths are cast,
And the blue gentian-flower, that, in the breeze,
Nods lonely, of her beauteous race the last.
Yet a few sunny days, in which the bee
Shall murmur by the hedge that skirts the way,
The cricket chirp upon the russet lea,
And man delight to linger in thy ray.
Yet one rich smile, and we will try to bear
The piercing winter frost, and winds, and darkened air.

William Cullen Bryant

Our northern November day itself is like spring water. It is melted frost, dissolved snow. There is a chill in it and an exhilaration also. The forenoon is all morning and the afternoon all evening. The shadows seem to come forth and to revenge themselves upon the day. The sunlight is diluted with darkness. The colors fade from the landscape, and only the sheen of the river lights up the gray and brown distance.

John Burroughs

The stillness of the woods and fields is remarkable at this season of the year. There is not even the creak of a cricket to be heard. Of myriads of dry shrub oak leaves, not one rustles. Your own breath can rustle them, yet the breath of heaven does not suffice to. The trees have the aspect of waiting for winter. The autumnal leaves have lost their color; they are now truly sere, dead, and the woods wear a sombre color. Summer and harvest are over. The hickories, birches, chestnuts, no less than the maples, have lost their leaves. The sprouts, which had shot up so vigorously to repair the damage which the choppers had done, have stopped short for the winter. Everything stands silent and expectant. If I listen, I hear only the note of a chickadee,—our most common and I may say native bird, most identified with our forests,—or perchance the scream of a jay, or perchance from the solemn depths of these woods I hear tolling far away the knell of one departed. Thought rushes in to fill the vacuum. As you walk, however, the partridge still bursts away. The silent, dry, almost leafless, certainly fruitless woods. You wonder what cheer that bird can find in them. The partridge bursts away from the foot of a shrub oak like its own dry fruit, immortal bird! This sound still startles us. Dry goldenrods, now turned gray and white, lint our clothes as we walk. And the drooping, downy seed-vessels of the epilobium remind us of the summer. Perchance you will meet with a few solitary asters in the dry fields, with a little color left. The sumach is stripped of

The Rapture of the Year

While skies glint bright with bluest light
Through clouds that race o'er field and town,
And leaves go dancing left and right,
And orchard apples tumble down;
While schoolgirls sweet, in lane or street,
Lean against the wind and feel and hear
Its glad heart like a lover's beat—
So reigns the rapture of the year.

Then ho! and hey! and whoop-hooray!
Though winter clouds be looming,
Remember a November day
Is merrier than mildest May
With all her blossoms blooming.

While birds in scattered flight are blown
Aloft and lost in dusky mist,
And truant boys scud home alone
Neath skies of gold and amethyst;
While twilight falls, and echo calls
Across the haunted atmosphere,
With low, sweet laughts at intervals,
So reigns the rapture of the year.

Then ho! and hey! and whoop-hooray!
Though winter clouds be looming,
Remember a November day
Is merrier than mildest May
With all her blossoms blooming.

James Whitcomb Riley

everything but its cone of red berries.

This is a peculiar season, peculiar for its stillness. The crickets have ceased their song. The few birds are well-nigh silent. The tinted and gay leaves are now sere and dead, and the woods wear a sombre aspect. A carpet of snow under the pines and shrub oaks will make it look more cheerful. Very few plants have now their spring. But thoughts still spring in man's brain. There are no flowers nor berries to speak of. The grass begins to die at top. In the morning it is stiff with frost. Ice has been discovered in somebody's tub very early this morn, of the thickness of a dollar. The flies are betwixt life and death. The wasps come into the houses and settle on the walls and windows. All insects go into crevices. The fly is entangled in a web and struggles vainly to escape, but there is no spider to secure him; the corner of the pane is a deserted camp. When I lived in the woods the wasps came by thousands to my lodge in November, as to winter quarters, and settled on my windows and on the walls over my head, sometimes deterring visitors from entering. Each morning, when they were numbed with cold, I swept some of them out.

But I did not trouble myself to get rid of them. They never molested me, though they bedded with me, and they gradually disappeared into what crevices I do not know, avoiding winter. I saw a squash bug go slowly behind a clapboard to avoid winter. As some of these seeds come up in the garden again in the spring, so some of these squash bugs come forth. The flies are for a long time in a somnambulic state. They have too little energy to clean their wings or heads, which are covered with dust. They buzz and bump their heads against the windows two or three times a day, or lie on their backs in a trance, and that is all,—two or three short spurts. One of these mornings we shall hear that Mr. Minott had to break the ice to water his cow. And so it will go on till the ground freezes. If the race had never lived through a winter, what would they think was coming?

Henry David Thoreau

I have frequently been surprised, in late fall and early winter, to see how unequal or irregular was the encroachment of the frost upon the earth. If there is suddenly a great fall in the mercury, the frost lays siege to the soil and effects a lodgment here and there, and extends its conquests gradually. At one place in the field you can easily run your staff through into the soft ground, when a few rods farther on it will be as hard as a rock. A little covering of dry grass or leaves is a great protection. The moist places hold out long and the spring runs never freeze. You find the frost has gone several inches into the plowed ground, but on going to the woods and poking away the leaves and debris under the hemlocks and cedars, you find there is no frost at all. The Earth freezes her ears and toes and naked places first, and her body last.

John Burroughs